HAT TRICKS & CHRISMUKKAH NIGHTS

A HOLIDAY SPARKS ROMANCE

EVEY LYON

TYLER & LAINEY'S PLAYLIST

Halloween by Novo Amor

Crash Into Me by Petey USA

Northwestern Girls by Say Hi

Wildest Dreams by The Native

When I Get Home For Christmas by Snow Patrol

Let It Snow by Kacey Musgraves & The Quebe Sisters

Jingle bell Rock by The Rogue Wave

Christmas Wrapping by The Waitresses

New Year's Day by Taylor Swift

Stay At Home by Laney Jones

Come Away by Nini Camps

Itshitfuq by Meg Elsier

Opaline by Novo Amor

Teeth by Mallrat

CHAPTER 1
TYLER

*D*on't take the chocolate one with nuts. Don't do it, kid.

I watch as two little hands dig into the bowl of candy that I'm holding. Of all the options in the bowl, his little claws grab onto the bar that I want. But then my eyes draw up from my loss of candy straight to a little seven-year-old boy with a wide grin and a robot hat on his head, covering his brown mop of hair. Ah, give the boy two. I dip my hand in the bowl and grab another one for him. I peer around his shoulder to his mother.

I shouldn't find her cute as fuck, with her dark red scarf shaping around the bottom of her face, nearly breathtakingly beautiful. Autumn suits her. Her brown hair and dark green sweaters bring out her brown eyes.

Fuck it. She. Can. Not. Make. Me. A. Sappy. Human.

Her scowl is in full force today, so I ceremonially dump the entire bowl of candy into the boy's pillowcase sack knowing very well his mom will hate having an extra month's worth of Halloween candy for him to nag her about.

Most people think I'm a total asshole. They could be

right, but it gets the job done when I'm out on the ice, eager to reach the puck before an opponent. Off the ice, I *might* have a few days which are not exemplar, either. It makes zero sense to most as to why I am this way, as I come from a loving family.

My dad owns a big marketing firm in Chicago, and my mom is a graphic designer. Humor has always been front and center in our family. Hell, they even named my big sister Luna after a psychic who once read them their apparent future. I mean, the psychic wasn't half wrong, but still. Our family is supportive of one another, and I'm close with my parents. They support my hockey career even though they still don't even understand the game's rules.

I should be a good guy. Doesn't mean I am. And right now? Am I being a total jerk for the sake of pissing off my neighbor? Maybe.

The woman in question clears her throat, snapping my gaze from the little robot to her tight jawline. "Enzo, what do you say?"

"Whoa, this is super cool. Thanks, Tyler." My seven-year-old neighbor is in his Halloween glory. He already has half a pillowcase of candy. But he also always looks at me with admiring eyes. I'm Tyler Ives, the hockey player. That means something to him.

"What manners you teach your son, Lainey." I smile contritely at the woman of my contempt.

Her lips twitch, eyes spearing into me, and her arms are crossed, pushing up her tits. Because, yeah, I notice.

"Imagine that. Politeness and a happy face. It goes a long way, you know," she volleys back.

I lean against the pane of my front door in our apartment building while Enzo skates his gaze between his mom and me.

"Ah yes, Lainey reminding me that I'm a grumpy, insufferable human. Makes my day complete." I place my large hand against my heart. She annoys me to the max because she points out what my mother constantly repeats… don't be so cranky, smile, lighten up. I don't need constant reminders.

She touches her son's shoulder and sighs. "Enzo, why don't you head on inside." She quickly takes a few steps back to unlock their front door with her key. Then she points her finger at him with a warm smile that is admittedly good to see. "And don't you dare steal a piece of candy yet," she warns him sternly, with her smile not evaporating a single bit.

Enzo groans while he treads across the hall into the apartment. When he closes the door behind him, Lainey zips her sharp look to me.

We have a few seconds of a face-off as we normally do. It was like this from moment one. Lainey moved in a few months ago, taking over the apartment from her brother when he got traded to Anaheim. Seb and I were civil for the sake of the team, but if given the choice, then we probably would've dropped the gloves a time or two. We both, however, could agree on one thing, which is that the small-town life is more our thing, which explains how we both ended up in Everhope in Lake Spark country, where I'm a forward for the Spinners that train one town over. Just so happens there are only so many apartments renovated warehouse-style designed to choose from.

His sister? She's hated me from day one purely by my association to hockey. I know enough about her since she's been to a few team functions. I quickly learned that she's been a single mom basically since Enzo was born. Seb stepped in as a male role model, and that I admire. But he's no longer here. Still, Enzo seems happy, and I'll give that credit to Lainey.

And right now? I'll give credit to my in-season workout regimen as to why she is nibbling her bottom lip while her eyes appraise me.

Licking her lips, she snaps out of her state that makes me a little cocky. "Nice play the other night. Might want to learn how to win."

My eyes nearly pop out at this woman's audacity. "Whoa. Hitting below the belt right away?" Thanks for the reminder of our not-so-stellar start to the season. She's an absolute Jezebel.

She can't help but smirk to herself. "The truth hurts."

I propel myself away from the door, quickly setting the empty bowl on the side table before I take a few strides toward her, causing her body to straighten and breath to hitch. It shouldn't excite me to see her this way, but I could make this a hobby that I enjoy.

"Why don't we just focus on the fact that Halloween is now thankfully over, and I swear if you put anything remotely wreathy near my front door then I will burn it in the fireplace. Your holiday cheer is fucking annoying."

I can tell she's desperately attempting to hold in a laugh. "You know we have Thanksgiving first, but Christmas wreathes will make an appearance. Maybe tinsel is more your style. Or does that give the impression you're too fluffy and soft for your latest conquests."

I swipe my hand through my hair and blow out a breath. She's really testing me today. How do I reply to that? I could highlight that I don't bring conquests home, but then it might highlight that I haven't slept with anyone in a long time.

"Believe anything you want." I decide to change our tone. "Listen, I'm away for a game tomorrow. So, you just celebrate that little fact of my absence, and maybe when I return..." I take one step closer and lean down until my mouth is near her ear. I choose to ignore the smell of candy in her hair, but the heat of her skin meeting my breath, that I notice. "You can play nice," I whisper firmly.

Oh yeah, she just shivered and in my favor.

Lainey shifts her head to the left to keep our faces far too close and her mouth in dangerous proximity to my own. "Says…" she rasps in a sultry way that I would spank her for, and that thought alone shouldn't be in my head right now. "Satan."

There it is. Her ever-so-kind retort.

We step back from one another and take a breather. Our eyes remain locked for a few seconds before I decide that I need to leave this hall and enjoy an evening of peace and rubbing one out.

"Night, Lainey, may your dreams tonight be of clowns or some shit that scares the hell out of you."

"Funny." She rolls her eyes.

After a few more seconds and a slip-up of staring at her lips for a moment, I turn to head inside.

"Tyler, wait." Lainey's voice softens, and it causes me to glance back at her. She sighs a breath while her eyes flicker closed then open. "Thanks." Appreciation floods her face as I turn and fold my arms over my chest. She points to the pumpkin by my door that Enzo gave me last week. "I mean, I know these holidays must be your idea of hell."

"They are," I confirm sharply.

"And your heart probably struggles with the festive joy of the months from October to December, questionable if January first falls into that timeframe."

"I don't have a heart," I mundanely point out.

She tries to look anywhere but at me. "It's just… I'm aware of all of that, and I just wanted to say… thanks." Her eyes flick up to meet mine.

Ah.

Maybe it started a month ago when I left tickets for Enzo to see a game because I overheard him talking to his mom in the elevator, excited about hockey but bummed his uncle wasn't around to get tickets for a team no longer his.

Or maybe it's the way he told me about his costume for weeks whenever I ran into them in the parking garage.

"It's no problem." I mean it sincerely.

The corners of her mouth tug, and I wouldn't need a magnifying glass to see that she nearly gave me a little smile. She gives me a little nod before disappearing back into her place.

I can't help but watch her door close.

Any holiday, I hate. Except, I made an exception for ten minutes, and she just thanked me for a simple reason; for Enzo or her, I'm not quite sure.

Enzo is a great kid, and I can't seem to say no to him.

Despite my dislike for Halloween, I got candy for trick-or-treaters. Only one, actually. Because there was no way I was opening my door more than once. But Enzo asked last week right after he gave me a pumpkin if he could trick-or-treat at my door. It wasn't in my plan. Lainey pointed out to him that I was too cranky for that kind of stuff.

Still, I went out and bought candy to hand out.

Only for him.

And Lainey didn't even ask me to.

CHAPTER 2
LAINEY

Frowning, I watch as the barista takes down the paper ghosts hanging in the window while her other colleague begins to wrap green garland and holiday lights along the window looking out on Main Street.

"They waste no time," I comment.

A chirp of a laugh brings my attention to my best friend, Gracie. She's sitting across from me at our small corner table. Her perfectly shaped red nails are a contrast to the white mug of coffee that she's sipping on.

"It's okay. We still get to have pumpkin spice lattes for another month. Thanksgiving allows it," she reminds me.

I lift my mug of chai with a fresh cinnamon stick poking out. "A shame you are missing Thanksgiving this year." She's spending it with her family and won't be home.

Gracie lifts a shoulder. "It's okay. We still have our annual holiday cookie-making night. That reminds me, I need to find some new Hanukkah cookie cutters." She's been my friend since we were kids. Her dad used to be a big-name football coach but now enjoys a quiet life in Lake Spark, plus he's a huge sponsor for the Spinners hockey team. Most people think she is probably spoiled, but she has the kindest heart and is talented in her own right so will take over her mom's boutique one day. A lingerie boutique, but Gracie has a talent for dresses.

"I can't believe that we survived last year's bake-a-thon." We bake basically every recipe we have for holiday treats then box them into containers to give to friends and family. Enzo loves it and looks forward to it every year.

Gracie squints her eyes at me and seems to be formulating a thought. "Since I won't be at Thanksgiving, then there will be an empty seat at your table." She brings her finger to her chin. "Hmm, who might fill that seat since there's no hockey game that day."

I throw her an immediate death stare. "Funny." Gosh, why am I thinking about the cocky grin and arrogant demeanor that complements his maybe-sexy, darkish hair and piercing eyes? What a jerk for slipping into my thoughts.

She sets her coffee down and rests her elbows on the table to bring her fists up under her chin, clearly wanting to gossip. "Why not? I mean, Tyler pisses off most of the team, but you must be chipping away at his steely little heart."

"Exactly, steely."

"Did he not leave tickets for Enzo for the game a few weeks back?"

The tiny lift inside my chest from the reminder of what he did hits me for a millisecond. "I'm sure handing out tickets is as easy as throwing a coat on. Not much effort." Not exactly, but fine.

She raises her brows at me. "And Halloween?"

Now my chest expands more than I would like. "It… it… was for Enzo." And I appreciate it. Whatever hostilities may exist between us, he doesn't take it out on my son.

"Maybe. But it was sweet. Not many men know how to deal with the kids of a hot mom who lives across the hall."

I sigh at the state of my life. From day one, Enzo's dad has been long gone. I met Jamie when I was in college studying to be a teacher. He was a very good player on the college hockey team, and we met at a party. We dated for a bit, but two months in, I got pregnant. I gave him a choice, and he took it. Said he had his hockey career to think about. He only plays in the minors now, so his star-player dreams didn't exactly pan out.

Maybe it's my experience with Enzo's father that made me have a natural disdain for hockey players. My brother, Seb, is the exception, and I will always put on a happy face when he drags me along to events, but still, I don't have a high opinion of most players. They think they own the world and selfishly make their choices around their careers.

Besides, I'm focused on my son. I would like to think that I'm rocking it as a single mom, but I'm scared to admit that in case I'm wrong. I finished my degree just before Enzo arrived, my family has always been supportive, and I have a good job at the preschool in town. Hailey, the owner, is flexible, and I get to have better hours for Enzo. When my brother said I could take over his lease that he'd already paid the year for, I took him up on it. It was a no-brainer. I might be independent, but a safe place for Enzo is a non-negotiable for me, and free is a bonus.

Seb warned me about the neighbor situation but said he and Tyler just stayed out of one another's way. But something about Tyler just irritated me from day one. My innate instinct for players or maybe my brother's opinions were already too embedded into my brain. There is just one problem to my current life.

Enzo is crazy about Tyler.

Dating hasn't been in my cards for a long time. I always fear that Enzo will get attached and then get hurt when they don't stick around. I didn't plan on my neighbor being an attachment for him.

Or for my neighbor to be sinfully hot.

The tapping of nails on the table reminds me that Gracie is waiting for me to say something.

"He's just trying to stay civil in our hallway," I justify.

"Sure." She doesn't believe me. She wiggles on her chair while I sink into my own. "Lainey, let me be blunt. You should consider just fucking it out. A little hate sex can be fun."

My eyes bug out. "How the hell did we go from him being a kind neighbor to my son to me fucking my neighbor senseless?"

"See? You have thought about it. You are going for the hard-and-senseless style."

I try not to laugh, and I rub my temples. "Not happening." My eyes land on the piece of pumpkin bread on a plate that I forgot I had. I pull a little morsel off to take a bite. "Besides, I have zero time between now and New Year's. My to-do list is forever long."

"What about your naughty list? Is that long, too?" Gracie flashes her brows at me.

I throw the piece of food at her. "Stop it. Besides, you still haven't told me what happened the other night."

Her face falls, and she crosses her arms to lean back in the chair. "The new coach kind of happened. I'm not going to complain about that one single bit, but it was a one-time thing. I mean, not during the night because that was more than a one-time thing, but you know what I mean."

My mouth goes slack from her confession, as I had no idea. "Whoa, you say that so casually, but isn't it a big deal?"

Gracie is never shy and always candid, so it doesn't surprise me, it's just the unpredictability of what she says out loud sometimes that still causes my brain to have an instant reaction.

"What?" Her eyes grow wide. "Take opportunities when they arise. So, back to you—"

"Wait, does this mean you technically hooked up with Tyler's cousin?" Family coaching family happens sometimes in the pros.

She quirks her lips out for a thought. "Second cousin. But yeah. Small world. Back to you… again. You have an opportunity that literally is a few feet away from your front door." She brushes past her own situation that she clearly does not want to discuss.

I snort a laugh. "Nah. We don't do well with conversation, and to be honest, his entire demeanor causes me to believe he is probably an asshole when it involves sex too. The quickie then kick her out of bed kind of guy. That's not my style." My mind can't even envision any other way he might be in bed.

Gracie tilts her head side to side as she considers my thought process. "Fine. I will let it go… for today."

Shaking my head, I smile to myself because her pursuit is humorous. "Anyhow, I need to start shopping for Santa. Enzo wrote his list the day after Halloween. The usual, cars, hockey stuff, and a few books to my surprise. I love this season." It always brightens my mood. "But there is one thing I hate."

Gracie and I look at one another. "Gift wrapping," we say in unison then giggle.

She glances at her watch and quickly takes her last sip of coffee before she stands. "I have to go. I have family dinner later and helping my parents drag out holiday decorations from the garage. I will just supervise that." Her family celebrates Hanukkah and Christmas and have a talent for taking Chrismukkah to a whole new level.

"No problem." I also stand and throw my scarf on. "I need to head to the grocery store before I pick up Enzo from school."

"Be sure to get extra soup for your neighbor." She winks at me while she buttons her coat.

"Why would I do that?" I play along.

Sliding her purse strap over her shoulder, she gives me a strange look. "Oh, I thought you already knew."

"Knew what?"

"Tyler is out for the next game. In last night's game, he got a nasty blow when a player skated into him."

I shrug. "And? He plays hockey. It happens. My brother gets hit all the time." Doesn't make it any easier. You're always scared that it will be a serious one.

"True. But he full-on had to leave the game after a hit to the face. He won't be playing the next game."

Her news piques my interest, and a flare of concern erupts in a corner somewhere inside of me. "Oh? That doesn't sound great."

Gracie reaches out for a hug. "Yeah, looked painful. Anyhow, have fun. Give the kiddo a hug for me."

Squeezing her tight, I promise I will.

For the most part, I didn't think about what Gracie said because I was in full-on mom mode when I left the café. It was grocery store, school pick-up, drop books off at the library, and unloading groceries.

Finally at home, I'm scavenging through the last bag when I remember that I left the new bottle of laundry detergent in the hallway because I could only carry so much inside at once.

I gently jog to the front door and open it to pick up the bottle. But as I'm mid-squat, I notice Tyler is returning home. He's walking down the hallway in his coat and with stubble on his face, looking a little the worse for wear. Yet still, the wave of dark hair across his forehead frames his dark eyes.

It slightly startles me. "Shit. Are you okay?" Instantly, I see the bruise on the side of his face.

"Lainey, I'm not in the mood for your spats." He sounds completely deflated.

"I-I…" Slowly I straighten to standing, but my feet don't want to move. "Really. Truthfully. Are you okay?" All hostility aside, I'm genuinely concerned.

He peers down. "Fine. It will be fine. Just need ice."

"Yeah, ice. I guess you've done this a few times." My eyes slide back to my open door because looking straight at him might have me entranced.

"Something like that." He rubs the back of his neck.

Our eyes catch for a second, and a heaviness floats between us.

"I should let you be then," I say gently.

"Yeah." He is barely audible.

We both turn and head into our apartments, and for an unexplainable reason, I walk to the kitchen, slam the detergent on the kitchen counter, open the freezer, then half a minute later find myself knocking on Tyler's door with a bag of frozen peas in my hand.

By the third knock he opens, and his face squinches because he is surprised it's me. Let alone holding up a bag of frozen peas.

"Here." I hand them to him. "I wasn't sure if you have enough ice. I can only imagine your shoulder and upper body are a little effed up too. I remember because I've seen it on Seb."

In a quick movement, Tyler grips my wrist, and he yanks me forward until I almost tumble straight into him as I'm caught by surprise.

This is the complete wrong time for the ache between my legs, but it's happening.

He's strong but it's not enough to hurt. I stare up into his dark eyes as he towers over me. He steals my breath, and maybe that's the misery that he wants to inflict on me.

We just stew in this standoff for a few moments. I swear, with one more pull, our lips would be dangerously close. He has my eyes captivated because I see him searching for some sort of answer on my face.

"Thank you." His voice is gruff.

Make no mistake, I sense the electricity between us.

But he abruptly lets my wrist go, and I'm standing there speechless with my body trying to stabilize.

Taking a step back in disbelief, I'm unable to study his expression because the door slams in my face as I stand there at a loss for what I'm feeling in this very moment.

I'm angry that he causes something to stir inside of me, and I'm angry it's him because he is the last person I need in my romantic life.

The only thing I can do is punish him for that.

So tomorrow, I'll find holiday decorations for his door that I'm well aware he will hate.

CHAPTER 3
TYLER

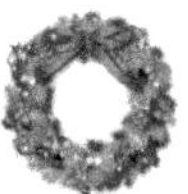

Carrying my dry-cleaned suits, I exit the elevator. I'm trying to see the bright side. After a week of missing practices, I've been cleared for practice tomorrow which means that I will most likely fly with the team for our game against Buffalo.

It takes one glimmer in the corner of my eye to make me do a double take.

"Fucking no," I grind the words out to myself.

I don't even need to wonder who took it upon themselves to add silver garland above my front door. Or a wreath with a giant red bow. Someone is crossing lines today, and I'm not in the mood for this blatant disrespect of my property.

I toss my dry cleaning over my shoulder with the hanger on my hooked finger and basically stomp straight to Lainey's apartment. My fist lands on the door for a strong knock, then another, and another.

The door rushes open. "Okay, okay. I got the message the first time." She seems slightly disheveled from rushing to the door; she's wearing yoga pants and a long-sleeve shirt that hugs just under her shapely ass. When her eyes follow a line from my middle up, her face melts into recognition, and a sly smile even begins to curve on her mouth.

"Cut the crap. No, even better, take some scissors and cut down the decorations on my door."

She sets her hands on her hips, completely in her element of enjoying a win. "Oh." She fakes a pout, and for some reason, I make a mental note that her lips are the perfect shape for activities that I shouldn't consider doing with this woman, unless it's to release some of our bizarre tension. "Someone isn't in a festive mood. I forgot Scrooge's cousin is my neighbor."

"Cute. Now take it down."

Her eyes assess me for a second or two, and her proud accomplishment disappears. "I just thought you might want a little holiday cheer, and Enzo and I took the liberty of checking it off your to-do list."

"Oh. Didn't think of asking me first?" I reply flatly.

She holds her long finger against her thumb in the air. "Maybe there is a little smidgen of me that knew it would piss you off."

My eyes skate to the side, and I roll my lips in. "Oh, what a surprise." I'm flippant. "Please take it down."

Her eyes squint again, and she seems to be studying me. I don't like that. "Why do you hate the holidays so much?"

"It's not that hate them, per se. It's more that I don't have time for this sparkle shit. I have games during the holiday period."

"Liar. You have three days off at Christmas. Prime holiday time, don't ya think?"

Damn it. Of course, she knows the schedule. Her brother plays. And I hate the way she said *think* with the little pop and a knowing glare fixed on me.

I shrug my shoulders. "Aren't we a smartass today."

She smiles cheekily. "I am always."

I bite the inside of my cheek and take a moment to adjust to the fact that the decorations are going nowhere. "Fine. But you have to clean this shit up at the end of Christmas."

"New Year's. The holiday season ends after the first of the year, unless you would like us to include Three Kings Day on January sixth."

My eyes widen, warning her not to test me right now, even though I *might* be fighting a faint smile due to her humor today.

"Mom!" We both hear Enzo call out, and it is an alarming tone.

Without reluctance, Lainey runs into the apartment, leaving the door wide open behind her. My foot moves forward then back, hesitating about how involved I should be. Then again, a kid just yelled out, and it sounded urgent. I quickly turn back and hang my dry cleaning on my doorknob then dash straight back and into Lainey's apartment.

Only briefly do I notice that this place has a woman's touch, with candles and framed photos, and I nearly trip over a toy in the process of reaching Lainey and Enzo by the window in the living room.

"Is everything okay?" I ask.

Enzo smiles ear to ear and jumps as he points outside. "It's snowing! Look, Mom." He yanks Lainey's arm close.

She chirps a little laugh. "I see."

I can't help but half-smile to myself. Enzo is purely excited for the first snow of the year. We've had sleet already, but this is proper snow that sits on the ground. November snowfall is normal for Illinois. I used to be as excited as him when the first sign of winter was visible with flakes. It also meant that hockey season on frozen ponds had begun.

"We can go sledding!"

Lainey giggles and rustles her son's hair. "Need a little more snow than that."

"Can we build a snowman? We have carrots, right?" He is so enthusiastic that I forget about the fact Lainey butchered my door with garland.

"Still not enough snow for that, either," she confirms.

I take a step forward and peer up through the glass to the clouds. The flakes are by no means mere flurries. Soon there will be a sheet of snow on the ground. "Maybe later today," I note.

The sound of a *wow* becomes background noise as I consider if the snow will put a damper on my plans for tomorrow's practice and our team traveling out. I guess that's a day away.

"Please, Tyler?"

The sound of a pleading seven-year-old brings my attention back to the fact that I'm standing in Lainey's apartment. "What?" I must have missed the first part of his request.

"If there is enough snow later, will you help me outside? My mom sucks at pulling the sled, only my Uncle Seb used to be able to do it."

Lainey sets her hand on her son's shoulder. "Hey. We don't say suck. Don't make the swear and bad-word jar return."

Cliché.

"Besides, I'm sure Tyler is busy," she adds.

"Are you?" Enzo's eyes marvel at me, and his hands are laced together to beg.

"I am…" I glance to Lainey who stares at me strangely. "Today, I'm…" My voice grows uneven, but then I think logistically, and surely it won't snow enough for sledding by the afternoon, so I'm essentially off the hook. "Sure, kiddo." I smile at him.

He jumps up and down in excitement. "Awesome. I'm going to search for my sled."

Before Lainey can protest, he darts away at full speed, and she doesn't get a chance to pat his shoulder to calm him. She smiles nervously when she turns to me. "It's in the storage downstairs, but I'll let him figure that out." Her sleeves are around her knuckles, and she hugs herself. "You don't need—"

"It's fine." I give up.

We both stand there in silence, not sure what to say or where to look. I should be making my escape from the woman who drives me crazy in ways that are a headache to my brain and evil to my dick.

Her lips pinch, and she avoids my gaze. That's my cue to leave.

"I'll just…" Our eyes meet again as though she's waiting for something. "Go," I say to finish my sentence.

She nods. "Yeah, of course."

I begin to walk backwards, but I step on something sharp, causing me to lose my balance when I look. "Fuck."

Lainey steps closer and winces as she examines the floor. "Yeah, that's just the lava of death. Those little plastic blocks can be lethal even with shoes on. Sorry, Enzo was working on some spaceship or something… and it's a good thing we don't have the swear jar." She is trying to be lighthearted, and she gets points for that because the energy in here is indescribable and messing with my senses.

"Got it. Well, good luck with the spaceship, planet, pirate ship, whatever it is." *Because I can't think straight around the fact your face seems to glow today.*

"Sure. And you know, don't worry about snowmen and sleds," she tells me as she follows me out, letting me off the hook.

But suddenly, I don't like that for some reason. The idea that someone is letting Enzo down doesn't feel right. Glancing over my shoulder, I simply reply, "Just knock when it's time."

STANDING OUTSIDE with a hyped-up kid running around me, I can't help but grin. My theory that it wouldn't snow enough went out the window, and I'm now getting dizzy from Enzo unable to decide between snowman pursuits or giving me a workout by pulling him in the sled.

"Ready there, bud?"

He stops in his tracks and looks at me, his hat lopsided on his head. "Sled."

"Come on then." I pick up the rope attached to the sled while he hops on.

I begin to run and realize I need to manage my strength because I'm too strong and he will go way too fast. He's already squealing with joy by the time I'm ten seconds in. And so it goes for the next twenty minutes before we move on to snowman making.

A set of heavy eyes on me the entire time doesn't deter me, and sometimes I even forget that Lainey is watching while she sips from her thermos cup of coffee and occasionally takes a few photos of her son.

It's only when Enzo accidentally throws a ball of snow at her and it hits her just under her chin that chaos erupts. Lainey stands there in shock that she just became a target.

Her jaw drops theatrically at her son. "Watch out, otherwise I will get you back," she warns.

He just continues to giggle. "Sorry."

"Just let her be. Your mom can't handle snowballs." I guide him back to our snowman efforts.

But then I feel a cold ball hit my back, and slowly turning on my heel, I see that Lainey just proved me wrong as she proudly brushes her hands free of snow with her thermos at her feet.

"Really? You want to go down this road?" I double-check.

"I did nothing," she lies playfully.

A switch in me brings out a younger version of myself, and I lean down to sweep up snow to make into a ball then throw one back at her, aiming for her arm.

Then havoc begins. Enzo joins in, we are all chasing one another, Enzo and Lainey team up against me, then Enzo goes rogue and is after both Lainey and me.

Which is how Lainey and I end up lying on the snow trying to avoid a snowball. I'm nearly on top of her, and we both realize it. She's panting from running around and waits for her breath to calm. I make zero effort to move, including my arm around her waist as I lie on my side. Her eyes are milk chocolate today, and they are staking my own.

It would take one move and I could drop my lips to hers, and I'm concerned that thought crosses my mind, but attraction is attraction. Luckily, the idea exits my brain when Enzo arrives running. Lainey is quick to push me away, and she clears her throat. Standing, she brushes off the white powder.

"Time for a snack? Hot chocolate?" she suggests, as she must sense that he is tired.

"With whipped cream?" he asks, trying his luck.

"Yep."

She turns to watch me return to standing. "Would you like some hot chocolate?" She's gone shy, and it must come down to a moment that we shouldn't be having.

I raise my hand to stop her. "Nah. It isn't my cheat day, and I need to stick to my nutrition schedule for the season."

She tucks her hair behind her ear because her hat is doing a half-assed job of covering her ears. "Right. Forgot about that. Seb is the same way."

Also, I need to create space after today. It's twisting my wires, and I need to focus on hockey.

"I'm sure you would poison my drink anyhow," I tease her.

She bobbles her head side to side before playing with the end of the scarf. "Nah, my piss-you-off quota is full for the day."

Okay, she doesn't hate me that much.

"Good to know there is a quota." I hold her eyes prisoner longer than I should, and luckily, I'm saved when her son calls out for her.

I shouldn't need saving at all.

CHAPTER 4
TYLER

The guys leave the ice in an orderly way, which is surprising since we're all beat. Coach worked us hard. We've won our last three games, but he wasn't happy with our penalty kill the other night and felt we let too many soft goals through.

Didn't help that Smith ended up in the penalty box for a fight that didn't need to happen, and I followed three minutes later. In my defense, at the time it seemed logical. The ref should have called tripping but he didn't, so I took out a little anger.

"Ives." Coach states my name with the underlying tone that I better get my ass over, as he wants a word.

Asher Tate is new this season. He's fair, well respected, but takes no prisoners when it comes to compassion. It's worse because he's my older second cousin. The age difference is enough that we're not that close. I'm lucky that nobody thinks he gives me special treatment; if anything, he's harder on me. His brother, Shaw, is even on a rival team. Probably for the best, as he is wild. Besides, there is another team in the league where the coach has his son-in-law on the team. That's got to mean fucking awkward family dinners. Basically, having family in the same league isn't unusual.

Walking in my skates to the side where he stands by a bench, his look is unreadable as always. "You've been playing the best hockey of your career, but if you pull any more shit that lands you a penalty for unsportsmanlike conduct again, then I won't be pleased."

"Yes, Coach." Because I don't dare say his first name.

"We're lucky you were able to come back and play the other week after your injury, so let's not ruin it. Understand?"

"Yes, Coach." What else can I say?

He hums a sound and lifts his nose slightly. "I don't care about players' personal lives but consider actually taking a day off mentally on Thanksgiving. I can't have you on edge. If the other guys can do it, then so can you. Understand?"

I want to throw it back at him that he should take his own advice. Alas, all I do is sigh as I soak in his words. "I do."

"Good." His stoic face is unreadable.

Maybe I shouldn't poke the bear, but suddenly I feel ballsy today. "Uh, shouldn't you also take a mental day? I'm confident someone in the family is already plotting Chrismukkah, and that is an energy drainer. Although, the food is a solid ten."

He doesn't flinch and stares at me. "No. You always have energy for Sufganiyah with the right amount of jam inside." He remains serious. "Now, we have one more away game and then off a day before we head out again. Rest up."

"See you tomorrow."

Leaving him, I vaguely hear him return to his conversation with one of the assistant coaches. In the locker room, the guys seem to be in good spirits, only with a few discussing some plays.

Sitting down, I begin to untie my skates when Charlie sitting next to me bumps my arm.

He's been on the team for a few years now. He has a no-trade clause in his contract, so he basically can call the Spinners his home, as there is more stability.

"Everything good?" he checks in.

"Yeah. Coach being Coach. Need to keep my head in the game but rest, yadda, yadda." I pull off a skate.

He chuckles under his breath. "Makes sense. You are a little high-strung this time of year." Probably because my parents are busy as hell with their marketing firm in Chicago and then always suddenly decide that Christmas is the most important day of the year.

"I'm just waiting for my mom to drop the bomb that it's her usual festivity time."

"Fair enough. Hey, doesn't Seb's sister still live in your building?"

His question gets my full attention. "Yeah, why?"

He rolls a shoulder back. "Nothing. Just wondering."

"No, you weren't. So, what is it?"

He scratches his cheek while he takes a break from removing his pads. "Heard she was single. I mean, she has a kid, but the dad isn't around if I remember Seb mentioning once."

I still don't know the full story, and it's none of my business either. "Point being?"

"Maybe she can brighten your mood."

I rub a towel across my face. "Nah. I'm good." Though it might already be happening.

"Okay. Well, the missus wanted me to invite you to Thanksgiving dinner."

"Thanks, but I think I will just take a down day and call

my parents. They wanted me to drive out to the city, but they will have to settle with a simple call."

He stands and looks at me, unimpressed. "Geez. That sounds miserable. Well, if you change your mind."

I give him a nod. "I know where to go."

Charlie walks toward the showers, and for some reason, it feels as though I stay behind to wallow.

But I get my shit together, and thirty minutes later, I'm dressed and stop in town for a coffee. As much as I hate this time of year, it would be a lie if I said it didn't hit different on Main Street. The atmosphere seems to cause people to be extra friendly, and the twinkly lights are not all that bad. I consider running into one of the boutiques. I do most of my shopping online, but my mom is crazy about the candles in this store up on the corner. Special scented or something like that.

As if she has a sixth sense, my phone vibrates, and fishing it out of my pocket with one hand, I see her name across the screen. Hitting accept, I bring the phone to my ear and say hello.

"There's my son who is horrible at communication and leaving his dear old but young mom wondering if he is still alive and not eaten by a pack of wolves." She is teasing me because she can never be mad.

I smile wryly. "Sorry. I've been busy with the season."

"Yeah, yeah, yeah. You played a good game the other night, but that's all the hockey talk you'll get. Your dad is wondering if he can ship you more Matchbox mezcal or beer for gifts to your friends."

"Geez. I know my uncle owns the company, but that doesn't mean I need to stockpile in my home. He's doing well enough. Doesn't need me to advertise the brand." He's doing more than alright. For years, my uncle Max and his friends have had a little investment in the Matchbox brand of mezcal and beer. They signed a pretty hefty distribution deal way back, and of course, I volunteered to do a few social media posts for them, but my services are done.

I can picture her warm smile on the other end. "Listen, I know Thanksgiving is a no-go with your schedule. Your aunts and uncles, cousins, and everyone remotely related will miss you at dinner. Maybe we can do a family call? Anyhow, we don't get you for Thanksgiving, but maybe Christmas?"

"I don't know. I kind of just want to take it easy. Our schedule has been a killer, with a lot of back-to-back games."

"I'm your mom, so I don't really have to ask, but I thought I would anyhow. Since you won't take the drive to Chicago, then maybe we'll come to you. Your sister couldn't swing enough time off to make her trip from Amsterdam worth it." My older sister Luna is the apple of their eye and can wrap my dad around her finger in record time, but she is currently living abroad for a six-month job assignment. "Would you like it if we show up? Or will you play nice and invite us?" Now I'm grinning because Layla Ives takes no prisoners, all while she smiles, satisfied.

"Maybe."

"Well, that's better than a no. Now what about Thanksgiving? Please do something. Surely a teammate is hosting a dinner."

If I had a free hand, then I would rub my face in exasperation, but alas. "Yeah, one of the guys is doing something, so that's an option. I'm just going to see what I feel like."

"Okay. I'll check up on you to make sure you don't stay home all day."

"Got the memo. Need to run. Have Fun. Talk soon," I list then hang up. I'm sure I will get a text in five seconds that I forget to say I love you.

Taking a sip of my coffee, I continue my walk only to stop in my tracks when I nearly collide with Lainey and Enzo leaving the butcher's.

"Whoa." Lainey stands on her toes and hollows her stomach to prevent herself from running into my cup of coffee.

I step back. "Saved."

"Tyler!" Enzo is his usual happy self.

"Hey, kiddo."

"You rocked in the last game. You got sent to the box."

My brows furrow. "Wasn't it on way past your bedtime?"

"Yeah, but Mom let me watch you. Normally she doesn't, but she said it was fine."

I zip my sight to Lainey whose face I could swear is turning a shade of red. She pulls Enzo until his back is against her front. "Well, someone is talkative today."

"You two seem busy," I comment.

"Yeah, we were ordering our turkey."

Enzo is all smiles. "My mom makes the best Thanksgiving dinner. My uncle can't come, but my grandparents are."

"Yeah, well, hopefully. A few colleagues are stopping by, too," Lainey explains.

Enzo has another burst of energy and jumps up. "You should come to Thanksgiving." He turns to his mom. "Right? He is invited. He's our neighbor."

Lainey's mouth opens, but no words come out.

I pretend to drink a sip of coffee. I'm wrestling with the best way to get out of this. "You know, I think I'm just going to take it easy. A busy schedule and all."

"See, Enzo? Tyler is busy."

"But you've gotta have pie." Enzo seems deeply concerned.

Now I'm the one who has a frayed sound leaving their mouth because he is giving me no escape, it seems.

"Please. I mean, my mom can't even cut a turkey."

"Thanks." She is humorously offended.

I have to laugh at the kid's candidness. Enzo's attention travels between Lainey and me.

She notices her son's determination and gives me a subtle smile. "You're… welcome if you want to join."

To my surprise, that sentence was dripping with sincerity.

For a moment, I recall what Asher and my mom said. Maybe I need to have a mental day off.

It's just that I kind of fear that being around Lainey and Enzo are a different kind of mental obstacle, some spark of life that I didn't know existed.

Yet I'm unable to willingly escape.

All I can say is, "Maybe I'll stop by, Enzo."

That's the safest option. No commitments.

CHAPTER 5
LAINEY

I scrub the pot that I used for mashed potatoes aggressively. I'm completely pissed off. With the weather, for one. My parents didn't make it out, just like half of the country who were stranded with grounded flights. The colleague who was going to join us called to say she is sick. And the real reason that I'm probably frustrated with a sponge is because of my neighbor.

It's not that I had expectations, but Enzo was still hopeful that Tyler would stop by. It has not been my finest of days. Between nearly burning a turkey and crying my eyes out in my bathroom because I want Enzo to have a great Thanksgiving, I've given up. Enzo and I ended up eating dinner in our pajamas on the sofa while watching a movie.

I love autumn. The crunchy leaves, the colors, the family meals, and first snows. It's a season of change, and Thanksgiving warns us that it will officially be winter soon. I want everything to be perfect for Enzo, so I'm a little bummed about today to say the least.

My cell begins to vibrate on the counter near the sink, and I see my brother's name. Throwing the sponge into the sink, I quickly look for a towel but give up, and I lean down to touch my screen with my elbow. To my surprise it works.

Putting him on speaker, I continue to scrub. "Hey there," I say.

"Will you put me on video? It's a holiday."

I chuckle under my breath. "Not happening. I look like a hot mess." I find the towel and pick it up.

"Yeah, I hear Mom and Dad got stuck." There is sympathy in his voice. "I wish I was there, Sis. Also to see Enzo."

"I can get him."

"I'll call again later. I'm about to head into the team captain's house for dinner, and I just quickly wanted to check in."

He's sweet that way. "Thanks, big brother."

"Try to relax. There is no need to have high expectations for today. You can take it easy."

Sighing, I wish I could accept that feeling, but I can't. "Easier said than done, but I hear ya. I'll try my best."

"Good. Now I gotta run. I hope to make it work for Christmas so I can see you. Maybe I can fly you and Enzo out?"

"I'm sure he would love it, but we'll need to see."

"Okay, and your neighbor hasn't been a pain, has he? I'm scared to ask."

That's what has me triggered. "He's fine. No issues," I lie.

We say our goodbyes, and I hang up then instantly throw the nearby towel across the kitchen. I growl because I'm angry. It's my neighbor that *is* the issue.

How stupid of me to think that a hockey player would give a damn and put in some effort for a little boy who practically begged him to stop by. But *no*, Tyler is probably wallowing in his apartment with a beer and pizza.

This whole day just confirms that hockey guys are unreliable and selfish, and why am I hearing the doorbell?

Wait, what?

I can hear Enzo's thumping run from the living room to the front hall.

I quickly dash out of the kitchen. "Enzo, let me answer. You don't know who it—"

My son ignores me, and the door swooshes open. "Tyler!"

A few steps and I can see that my neighbor is standing in the hall. Now I'm furious because he has day-old stubble and that does things to a woman.

Crossing my arms, I watch as Tyler steps in because Enzo clears the way and smiles.

"I thought you wouldn't come. You've missed dinner, but we have loads of extras. My grandpa and grandma couldn't come because of the planes. My mom's mashed potatoes are not that great today, the turkey is okay-ish, but everything else is yummy."

I feign being offended with my mouth open. "Someone is a little honest today."

Enzo ignores me and pulls Tyler's wrist. Tyler glances over his shoulder back at me. "Just keeping you in check."

I roll my eyes to the side and close the door while Enzo tows our neighbor straight to the kitchen. I can hear my son talking without a break between sentences. He's excited.

I want to be relieved, but I also hate that I'm relying on someone to make Enzo's day. I shouldn't be able to stand the guy.

Following them, I admire how my son is already pointing to all of the food on the counter, cooling off in containers before heading to the fridge. "You're just in time. We haven't had pie yet."

Tyler seems overwhelmed but has a grin all the same.

"Why don't you take a breather," I suggest to Enzo. "I'll chat with our guest while you go check there are no tiny toy bricks on the ground for any of us to trip on."

My son grimaces at me before he marches off.

Silence fills the kitchen, and a whoosh of air travels through my body when it feels like Tyler turns to me in slow motion.

"It's, uh… I kind of assumed you weren't coming," I murmur.

He lifts a shoulder, then it sinks. "I said maybe."

I exhale loudly, annoyed. "Maybe isn't good for Enzo, or any kid." Leaning against the edge of the counter, I cross my arms, only to be reminded that I have ankle slippers, plaid pajama bottoms, and a form-fitting long-sleeve shirt that even I consider borderline too tight. My messy bun is questionable whether it's cute messy or not. Grumbling to myself, I can just add this to my day of mishaps. "It's not good for him to have any hope."

Tyler's eyes widen, and he leans against the island across from me. "Hope? I'm not sure Santa would be so happy that you are doubting it." Is he joking? Or is he trying to ease me into a conversation that isn't funny at all.

"I'm just saying. Be careful. He's my son and…"

"Listen, we got in late yesterday because of the travel havoc, and I needed sleep to function properly. Not my fault that half of this country thinks dinner at 2pm on this day is a good idea." He actually sounds kind of remorseful, and that takes me by surprise.

However, my mood has already been dampened, and my mind lets it go after a millisecond. "I'm just saying that Enzo is my number one, so maybes, no matter who it's from, causes momma bear to come out, and I should have known better because other than my brother, hockey players are all the same."

He seems taken aback by my tenacity and offended. His head tilts to the side, his face stoic. "You really want to be one of those people who believe in stereotypes? Because we're not all the same."

I stand taller, and I do my best to tamp down a rage building that shouldn't be seeing the light of day today. "You're all selfish and forget about others."

He steps forward, with his hands up to calm me. "Whoa there. You are a judgmental piece of work today," he chides. "I'm not sure why the hell I came now. After all, I'm an asshole who thinks only of himself."

He begins to turn, but I'm quick to grab his arm which causes him to pause, and his eyes drop down to my hand near his elbow before darting up to mine. It's as though he is searching for something.

"Wait… I'm sorry. I'm just a little on edge."

"No shit. You normally call me Scrooge, but you get that medal today."

My lips roll in while I try to take control of my thoughts. "Maybe."

"You hate that word, remember?" he deadpans.

Now my eyes grow slightly at his brazen response, and he only smirks cockily. "Just…" I squeeze my eyes shut for a second before opening them, with a calming breath that he probably heard. "Stay. Enzo is right. We have pie… a lot of it. Well, a lot of food, too, if you're hungry."

"Will you put on an apron and make me a plate?" Is he teasing me or is there a hint of… flirting?

I smile tightly at him. "Not a chance."

His gaze falls down. "Going to let me go now? Or will

your hand be holding onto me with this tight grip for the fore-seeable future."

My hand leaves his hard muscled arm as though he is fire and burned me. "Yeah, oh, sorry. I didn't mean to… you know… touch you." I'm rambling. Fuck. It just didn't cross my mind that I was even touching him; it's a natural touch, according to my body.

Tyler is clearly amused.

Making myself busy, I grab a plate and search the things on the counter. "I guess a bit of everything, right? I mean, it's a cheat day today, and I can imagine you need your protein and maybe some antioxidants, you know sweet potatoes have that."

"It's covered in marshmallows," he flatly points out.

"Sorry for being hospitable," I rebuke.

He slides onto a stool on the other side of the counter. "It looks good. I mean, the turkey looks a little dry, but you have cranberry sauce, so we're all good."

I'm exasperated, and it's audible. "Excuse me for not being up to your standards. See? Even on a holiday you're being a pain in the ass."

His chuckle vibrates through me. "Relax. It was a joke. You're a little uptight today."

"That's an understatement," I mutter under my breath.

"What was that?" I'm not sure if he heard me or not.

I shake my head gently while I load his plate with a spoonful of stuffing. "Nothing. It was nothing."

"Okay, as long as it's not another accusation of my hockey persona misconceptions." He pops a cornbread muffin into his mouth.

I grip the handle of the spoon a little harder. "Don't. Just don't bring it up."

"Fine. Can I at least ask why you have such a strong

disdain? I'm sure you have a dartboard with my face in the middle hidden in your room next to your toys."

My jaw drops, and I slide my gaze to him at his audacity. "What shitty manners you have."

"Ooh, shitty, I can imagine that word is on the swear-jar list." He grins smugly.

I point the spoon at him. "You really came here with no manners. I can't believe you just said that." Or that my face is burning right now.

"Gotta keep your low standards up," he rebuffs.

I growl under my breath then ceremonially drop a giant dollop of marshmallow-covered sweet potato on his plate, but it only causes him to smirk.

"You just have no idea, okay." I'm adamant that this topic needs to end.

Maybe he notices because suddenly he softens and swallows any retort he might have had for me. It's silent when I set the plate in front of him.

"Looks good. Thanks."

"You're welcome."

I decide now is a good moment to make a cup of tea before I shovel half a pie down my throat. Filling a pot with water and setting it on the stove, I feel his eyes on me. It should make me self-conscious, but I'm only more curious of what he is thinking.

"So, uh… your family. You're going to see them at Christmas or is that too much jolly joy for you?" I mundanely ask.

"Jolly joy is in our dictionary today?" He smiles wryly.

I shrug. "Could be. Anyhow, you're kind of related to the coach, right?"

"Yep, Asher is my second cousin. Plus, my dad's firm also represents a bunch of hockey sponsors."

"You don't sound thrilled *or* annoyed. You don't mind?"

He's busy cutting his piece of turkey when he lets out a sound. "Nah, it's fine. As long as nobody makes me feel as though I'm where I am because of connections or special treatment. So far, it's been okay. Asher and I keep things professional. And my dad? He wasn't one of those dads who put pressure on me or anything, either. Instead, he showed up to games and would get a little too zealous with the other hockey dads." Those memories make him smile to himself.

"Brothers and sisters?"

"A sister, Luna. I heard I was a handful as a kid, so I probably ruined their ideas of having any more," he jokes.

The pot is boiling, and I turn to pour the water into a mug with a tea bag. "I think Seb and I were pretty low-key. I'm not sure I'll see him this Christmas."

"My mom wants to visit."

I snicker a laugh. "Wouldn't that require a tree and holiday ham in the oven? You might lose your mind."

Tyler snaps his fingers. "Oh, but I'm so wise and would have her stay at the Dizzy Duck Inn and we can do dinner there. Plus, no ham necessary. My aunt is Jewish, and my mom's Christmas Day menu when she would visit kind of stuck with us even if she isn't visiting for the holidays."

"Interesting. And sending your parents to stay at a hotel? You really hate wholesome family time, don't you?" I swirl the teabag in my tea.

"I have hockey to think about. Other guys are good at balancing life and the game, but I'm not married, I don't have kids, so hockey can be my number one priority."

My mouth shuts tightly closed. Everything in that sentence was dripping with all the things I hate. A guy who puts hockey first.

If only he knew.

The sound of Enzo entering the kitchen luckily gives me the escape in my mind. "Let me guess. You are here for pie?"

"Yes. I've only been waiting like forever."

I walk to him and wrap my arms around his front to hug him from behind while we smile at Tyler. "He's so smart. Pie is always priority. And since my little guy ate his green bean casserole, then he most definitely deserves a giant piece."

"I don't know. I'm a big guy, I kind of need a lot of pie for my stamina. I might need half the pie, actually," Tyler says to my son, and that tiny blimp inside of me takes flight. The way he is with Enzo. Not a care that I've been a miserable host since the moment he stepped through the door.

"It's okay. You're going to need your strength when you have a game against my uncle later in the season."

Tyler hisses a whistle. "Watch it there, kiddo."

Enzo laughs while he heads to the pumpkin pie in the corner. I set my mug down and grab a knife from the drawer.

"I'll do it. The whipped cream is in the fridge. Meaning you need to go get it for me."

It takes a minute, but pie is dished out and everyone is happy eating sitting at the counter. Tyler engages Enzo in conversation about his latest theme at school which involves learning about the North Pole. I clean up, occasionally admiring the view in front of me that is a dangerous combination, because attachment does things to people, and it's my son that I need to protect.

But I keep letting Tyler in. I'm making no sense.

An hour later, Tyler informs my son that it's time for him to head out. He has an away game this weekend.

"Puzzles or your block creations. No more screen time," I call out to Enzo who disappears into the living room, but then I stall and wince to myself. "Fine," I give in. "It's a holiday.

Pick another movie." He didn't even need to ask, I'm soft today.

I trail behind Tyler until he opens the front door.

Taking over, I hold the door open, and he turns to me. Our eyes meet, and I'm not sure what to make of this second. It's different. That's for sure.

Especially when he reaches out and without hesitation slowly tucks a few loose strands of hair behind my ear, causing a soft tickle on my cheek.

"There," he rasps.

The entire area is closing in. My heart is hammering in my chest. What is he doing?

"Thanks," I whisper.

"No, thank *you*. It tasted good, and I was able to be kind of lazy and not touch my kitchen today," he quips.

I cluck my tongue. "Right. Because heaven forbid you actually wanted company today. You know that thing they call being social."

He winks at me, and it is so fucking sexy that I might drool. "Just following your stereotype protocol."

Yeah, that is on me. I deserved that.

I attempt to smile weakly, but it wilts quickly.

"Anyhow, night," he tells me.

I tip my nose up in acknowledgment then watch him cross the hall, the door closing behind him, and I'm wondering why the guy I should hate, just like every other guy whose career is on the ice, has me burning and melting into an unknown.

CHAPTER 6
LAINEY

I peruse the holiday market on a cold Sunday. Enzo is at a friend's, and I need to pick him up at 5.

"Candles. We need more candles." It's an insane thought because we do *not* need more candles.

In general, I love markets, but add the festive season and it just ups the ante. I step closer to a stall selling jars of jam and pick up the one labeled eggnog. My face screws up as I try to imagine that taste, and I'm not sure it's favorable.

"It's not as bad as it sounds," the old lady behind the table assures me and hands me a small tasting spoon.

I beam at her. "I'm sure it's delicious." Licking the spoon, I instantly want to gag, but instead, I give her an unsteady nod and smile. "Sure is." I swallow, attempting to get the taste out of my mouth. "Thank you. I'm just wandering around for now."

"I'll be here." She turns her attention to another patron while I walk away.

Inhaling a deep breath of the fresh cold air, I rub my gloved hands together. I'm relieved that all of Santa's gifts for Enzo have been clicked, with an email confirmation they are on the way. I can just focus on little things for friends and colleagues. It's easy since everyone's grateful for the thought.

Gracie would lose her cool and laugh all night if I were to get her the ornament that I see to my left that says *"eight crazy nights & one confused tree"*; it's amongst other options hanging on a small tree.

The sound of holiday music in the background fills the air, and up ahead, a blue stall is selling Hanukkah gifts. The *if life gives you potatoes, make latkes* sweatshirt is cute, although not that creative.

Up ahead I see the food truck selling coffee, and I'm sold. That is my priority since I haven't had a cup today. I was too busy with laundry and getting Enzo out the door to even remember. Prime example of why pets are not joining the family anytime soon.

I join the short line and check that they have my usual with oat milk. I shuffle through my purse for my wallet, and then I curse to myself when I remember that I left it in the car when I was filling the tank with gas. Fine. I'll quickly go to the parking lot and grab it since it isn't far.

The parking lot isn't that busy to my surprise. I guess people have school plays, holiday work parties they have to attend, or are simply decorating later than normal. When I'm at my car, I hit the key fob, and I'm about to open the door, but suddenly, a shift overcomes me. My body is on alarm when I feel someone behind me, and I turn to face them.

My stomach sinks because right in front of me is a reminder of everything I hate in life.

"Lainey," my ex's best friend says my name firmly.

Just like my ex, he is tall and slender, his hair a dirty blond and styled with gel. But right now, I'm surprised that he's standing in front of me.

"What are you doing here, Jones?" Maybe he hears how

uncomfortable I am in the moment. I refuse to let him notice my fear, but it's impossible. Doing my best to scan the area to see who is around, I fail because I'm trying to grasp why he is in front of me.

I haven't seen him in years, and I have no idea why he is here. I would like to remember that he has more sense than Jaime did. Maybe even a tad lower on the asshole scale, but he followed his best friend's cues, so I can only imagine that I am the devil in his world.

"My girlfriend dragged me down from Chicago to check out small town markets around Illinois. Boring as fuck, but here I am. I noticed you back by the coffee truck and dread filled me, just as much as you probably hate seeing me."

Standing taller, I feel my breath quicken. "Well, pretend you didn't see me."

I begin to step away, but he steps forward, trapping me between the car and him. My back hits the door of the car and he reaches out to wrap his hand around my arm.

"Wait, can we just talk for a second?"

My eyes grow, and I shake my head. "No," I state sharply.

"It's just… well… the situation."

"Let go of me. There is no situation."

His nostrils flare, and he glances to the side real quick then cuts his gaze right through me. "Lainey, we both know that's not true. I tried to tell him he was making a mis—"

"Fuck off, Jones. I don't care what your asshole friend and his family decided was best."

"Fair enough. Seeing you just kind of reminds me of all of that."

I struggle to leave his grasp. "All that? Right, the inconvenience I caused. Well, joke is on all of you because I have the best child humanly possible." Wiggling, I grunt my discomfort.

"Lainey, don't be so offensive. It all worked out."

"Then let me go."

Before Jones can answer, he is pushed to the side, freeing my arm. It happens so quick, but he ends up pressed against my car with an arm locking him in by his chest.

I blink a few times to understand the situation, but I see clear as day that it's Tyler.

"Don't fucking touch her," Tyler grits out.

"Relax. I was just trying to talk to her. We go way back."

Tyler only holds him down tighter. "And I don't fucking care. Don't threaten her or touch her, and even better, don't go near her."

Jones does his best to fight back, but it's useless. It's Tyler. His entire career is throwing people against the boards. "Dude, relax."

I attempt to touch Tyler's arm, because we don't need to waste time. But Tyler is too engrossed in his current state.

"I won't relax. When a woman says let her go, then let her fucking go. I have no problem killing a man for that. So don't get near her or I swear…"

"Tyler, stop."

His icy eyes slide to me, and he takes a breath before focusing on Jones and letting him go.

"Geez, man. What the hell is up with you?" Jones's gaze travels between Tyler and me while he rubs his shoulder. "Ah, I see. Well, Lainey and the kid are your problem now."

Tyler clenches his fists hanging at his sides, but luckily, Jones walks away like an animal who lost a fight.

I rub my face, taking in the last few minutes. The feeling of a soft hand on my arm brings my attention to the man in front of me who has concern written all over his face.

"Are you okay? Did he hurt you?" Tyler seems to survey my body.

"Yeah, I'm fine." But there is a mixed bag of emotions happening inside of me. I actually just want to cry.

"Who was that guy?"

"Long story. Why are you here?"

He rubs his palms along the length of my arms. "It's a maintenance day, so no practice, and it pains me to say it, but the market has knitted scarfs and jam that my aunt likes."

I try to stretch the line on my mouth because of his admittance, but I can't. I feel sick, and it's causing me to grow quiet.

"It's a good thing I was here. Who is that guy?" He is insistent on asking.

Ignoring his gaze, I try not to answer. I can't even comprehend because a hot tear pools in my eye. "I-I'm just going to go home." I begin to fumble with my key.

Tyler blocks me when I pivot on my feet. "Not like this you're not."

"I'm fine. Really. Let me just go home."

He sighs reluctantly. "It's a short drive. I'll follow you in my car."

"You don't…" I peer up to his face that is filled with worry. "Okay."

I guess he'll be waiting for me there.

CHAPTER 7
TYLER

I saw red.

That's what happened the moment I saw Lainey in the distance.

A beast inside of me came out with an automatic instinct to protect her. I would do it again too.

I'm not exactly sure who the guy was or why Lainey looks completely subdued while she slowly trudges toward her front door across from mine. I didn't say anything when we arrived back in separate cars; instead, I trailed behind her to watch that she is okay.

"Thanks." Her voice is barely audible.

"You should check your arm. You know, you can report him if you want." I'm not trying to put pressure on her, I just want to state the obvious.

Her droopy eyes look up to me. "It's not needed." She begins to fumble with her key, but I stop her and take the key from her with the intention to help.

"Not going to tell me who he was, are you?"

She sighs loudly and steps out of the way. "My ex's best friend."

Ah.

"Do you want to come in? For a coffee? I got a new machine a while back." I don't think she should be left alone right now.

She nods.

Following me into my place, it's when I notice her eyes soaking in her surroundings that I remember that she hasn't been inside my apartment before.

It's nothing crazy. I have high ceilings, large windows, and my kitchen has stainless steel appliances and an open-concept design. Admittedly, the stereotypical bachelor pad colors of navy blue and grays are the color scheme of my place.

Lainey settles herself on a stool by the kitchen island while I start up the machine.

"Any kind of coffee you want? You name it."

She rolls a shoulder back. "Just black coffee is fine."

Huh, I kind of took her for a latte kind of gal, but I guess right now she isn't in the mood for much.

"Coming right up."

She is silent while I sort out our coffees, and she shimmies off her coat. When I finally slide an Italian-sized cup in front of her, her eyes at last meet mine.

I say nothing and opt to wait patiently for her to say something.

I watch her take a sip, and she seems pleased with the taste. She begins with a sigh. "So yeah… that's my fucked-up day." Ah, she is bringing up what I witnessed.

"So, Enzo's dad?" My jaw flexes to the side.

"Jaime isn't part of Enzo's life, and neither is any of his family. I guess I was bound to run into someone from that former life. The world is only so big."

I circle the island to sit next to her on another stool. "Can I ask what's the story?"

Her cheeks puff from her large sigh. "The classic got pregnant in college and left alone. Jaime and I were only dating a couple months when it happened. He wanted me to end the pregnancy and so did his rich parents. I said no. So, he signed away his rights because a baby would have just gotten in the way of his hockey career. He barely made it into the minors, so not like he became a trophy winner."

A puzzle piece has just slotted into place.

I bite the corner of my lip, debating if I should prod the subject more. "Let me guess, his shitty behavior is why you hate hockey players?"

Lainey glances to the side then back to me. "Something like that."

"Don't let one guy ruin the world for you."

Her finger dances along the rim of her mug. "Trust me. I got more out of that situation than he did. But I would be lying if I said it doesn't hurt that Enzo doesn't have a father. I've been lucky that he hasn't really asked, but I know that time is coming soon."

"Is it that you truly believe that hockey is the reason he is a miserable son of a bitch or is it simply that it reminds you of the son of a bitch?" I swivel slightly on the stool.

She scoffs. "Maybe the latter," she admits. "But many players put hockey first, you even said it yourself the other day."

"Whoa, first off, having a baby is a different situation. Would I be thrilled? No. Would I take responsibility? Hell yeah."

Lainey presses her lips together while she listens.

"But this isn't about me. Are you scared that asshole from today will talk to your ex or say he's seen you?"

Her head drops slightly. "Not really. A year or two ago, my brother ran into Jaime's parents at a hockey benefit or something. They only reminded him how I ruined their son's focus. It took everything in Seb not to punch the dad. They all have zero interest." Her voice is shaky, and she's attempting to keep tears from falling.

I rest my hand on her shoulder to comfort her. "Their loss. You have a great kid, and when you put your witch's broom away, then you have some good days where you're a bearable human."

It earns me a little laugh. "Thanks… and thank you for being my superhero back there."

My fingers skirt up her arm and without thought land on her cheek. "No problem."

Her palm rises and covers my hand against her cheek. No words come to us, and instead, my thumb settles near the corner of her mouth and our eyes marvel in each other's. The sadness in her eyes begins to diminish, but her eyes glint due to the water of her remaining tears, laced with renewed light.

Slowly we both move. I feel the strong pull, and my own body gives up to gravity. I never want to admit it, but inside my head, I've said the obvious; she sometimes has me in a chokehold of attraction and interest in her personality.

I feel her breath mingling with mine, and then Lainey dives forward to kiss me. It nearly knocks me off the chair.

Our mouths meld together, and we kiss.

Her lips are firm against my attempt to be soft. We don't pull back, instead tilting the angle of our mouths. My hands move to cup her face as I kiss her, my mouth coasting hers, and her tongue sneaks past my lips.

I want to taste more of her, and the feeling of her hands snaking down my back gives me the sign that I can.

But it's whether I *should*.

Because as much as this kiss is better than I thought it would be, it can't be now.

Reluctantly I begin to pull away, but Lainey just attempts to kiss me more. It's only when I guide her back gently that our kiss breaks.

"Lainey, we can't."

She looks at me, shocked. "W-what?"

Standing up, I need to create space between us, or I'll just falter in my logic. I walk to the middle of the living room and begin to pace and scratch my head. "I mean, if you need a release in this moment to feel better, then fine. I can be that. But you're in a vulnerable place right now and…"

Lainey looks mortified, but also considering what my words are, she switches to angry. "Right. Got it." She abruptly stands and grabs her coat from the back of her chair. "I'm just a crazy mess right now, so of course, this is a mistake."

Gently shaking my head, I'm internally struggling if I'm handling this right. "It's not that. I just don't want to take advantage of you."

"This is not happening." She seems to be talking to herself, embarrassed. "Forget that I was even here. Or any of today. Of course, this is how this would end. You're all the same and just…"

My brows rise. "Just what?" She doesn't answer and turns to leave but then stalls with her back still to me. "Being the hockey player who has too much respect for you and won't take advantage of you? Because we're not all the same," I supply.

She doesn't say anything, and after a moment, leaves.

I drop my face into my hands.

My chest has been left in knots.

CHAPTER 8
LAINEY

The sharp knife cuts into the chocolate squares that are my specialty. They're melted chocolate and molasses then throw in some cookies and candy canes. With the casserole dish on the counter, I carefully divide the portions.

"So proud of you for using the Dash brand of molasses." Gracie brings her spatula to her heart because she is midway through taking the shaped holiday cookies off the cooling rack on the other side of the kitchen. Bear Dash is a local must. The owner of the hockey team also comes from a family that owns a famous syrup and molasses company.

"I think we are almost ready to do more decorating." I assess my kitchen that has every type of cookie, bar, and fudge known to mankind. It's our annual tradition.

I notice Enzo and Gracie with spoons scooping up the remaining cookie dough in the bowl.

"Hey!" I playfully swat him. "There is raw egg in that."

Splat.

My attention swings to Gracie whose spoon has fallen into the bowl at record speed.

Lines form on my head because this isn't Gracie; she would eat a whole tub if she could. "What's up with you? You always eat the chocolate chip dough."

"You know, I just decided that I'll focus on the powdered sugar for the puppy chow." She quickly grabs the plastic bag that holds cereal.

I'm puzzled by her weird demeanor, but when Enzo begins to whine, I refocus on him who hasn't listened, and I just give in and let him have one more bite before stealing the bowl away.

"It's not fair," he complains. "You and Auntie Gracie get to stay up and eat cookies."

I grab a tin to start distributing all our goods. "We are not eating them… *all*. And you already decorated a bunch of cookies; we are just going to finish the rest. So please, get ready for bed. You have school tomorrow."

He groans and begins to stomp away. "Fine." There is attitude in that voice.

"Don't forget the elf is watching and reporting to Santa every night," I remind him with my voice raised as he disappears around the corner.

Gracie chuffs a laugh as she plants herself down on a stool and grabs a bowl of icing to decorate the last of the snowflakes.

"We are almost done. I'll decorate the polar bear cookies." I grab one from the pile of dreidel- and stocking-shaped cookies, and instantly my face puzzles as I hold up the shape. "You didn't"

She smiles slyly at me. "Oh, I did."

"Seriously? I have young eyes in this home." I try not to burst out laughing that my friend made a dick-shaped cookie.

"It's holiday-themed. Maybe Santa is well-endowed. Or maybe your neighbor is." She smiles cheekily.

Instantly, my entire body sinks. I'm thankful that hockey season means Tyler comes and goes due to the game schedule. I've had a little escape. I updated Gracie on what happened as soon as I got home from making a fool of myself.

"I'm such an idiot," I mutter.

"You were in the moment and emotional. It happens. Kudos to him for putting a stop to it. See, chivalry isn't dead." She points the tube of icing at me.

Rolling my eyes, I throw her inappropriate cookie to the side and opt for a more classic-styled shape. "I just can't believe I did it."

"Let it go. Maybe he's forgotten about it. I mean, they've had like, what? Away game after away game. His mind might be occupied."

"Since when did you learn their schedule?" Something is up with her.

She chuffs a laugh. "I… I didn't… Only guessing." I give her a few seconds of my confusion as I try to figure it out before letting it go.

To be honest, I've only looked at the score of one of Tyler's games. Mostly, because I've been busy. It's prime craft season at school. We have a lot of December holidays to cover, using different-colored bottles of glitter.

"I think they haven't had the best of games, lately," I say.

"Meh, wins and losses. Inconsistent but better than last season. It comes down to Coach. He has to be firm but fair. But anyway, don't let it deter you. It's time for you to just get it over with. You'll run into him at some point, so be the one who is confident and in control."

I take a bite of a cookie and ponder her suggestion. We spend the next half-hour finishing up, and I leave her for a few minutes to put Enzo to bed. When I return to the kitchen, Gracie is busy closing a tin filled with goodies.

Her arm darts out, and she hands me the tin with a polar bear on it. "Here." I accept her offering. "I'll stay in case Enzo wakes up, but Tyler is back… so go."

My chin rises at my friend's words. "And you were thinking I can bring him cookies?"

"Tis the season, Lainey."

"I'm not sure it's a good idea."

She steps closer to me and tugs on my off-the-shoulder t-shirt, causing me to show more skin to be a little more brazen. "There. Now go say hello."

Gracie already has her hands on my shoulder and is turning me in the direction of the door before I can even protest. I'm basically shoved out the door, with it closing behind me.

Taking a big inhale, I pep myself up for this. She's right. This is no big deal, plus I have cookies. Who doesn't love cookies?

Still, I knock nervously on Tyler's door. I hear nothing, so I knock again. I wait for a few seconds then give up and feel partly saved. Turning around, I don't even get a chance to take a step because the door bursts open.

"I was in the shower, what do you want?"

Swirling back, I'm nearly blinded.

Oh no.

This can't be happening.

He has a towel hanging around his waist, and I can see his clearly defined stomach with lines that lead me down because the towel is low, tucked just below his belly button. Quickly, I swing my eyes away from him.

"Sorry. I just came…" That could be taken out of context. "I mean, I just came to give you something." I hold up the tin.

"What?" He doesn't sound impressed. Kind of grumpy, to be honest.

I brace myself and internally warn my eyes to focus on the only safe area… his face. But his chiseled jawline seems extra defined right now, and his eyes are piercing me.

"It's cookies, brownies, fudge, you know, that kind of thing. Happy holidays." I offer him the tin. "Just made them today. Maybe that's why you can smell them."

"Yeah, it's filling the hallway as if the building is suddenly a chocolate factory. Plus, I need to stay with my regimen."

I'm surprised by his demeanor. He's as cold as the weather outside.

"Okay, fine." I hold the cookies closer to my body again. "I also came to… apologize." I struggle to get the word out, and he doesn't reply nor flinch. "For the other night."

"You don't need to apologize," he says curtly.

My eyes flare bigger. "You're being an ass right now. I'm trying to come with a peace offering, and you don't even accept my cookies!"

"Maybe I don't want your cookies!" he argues back.

I puff out my chest, and it causes the fabric on my shoulder to lower even more. "Fine. Don't take my delicious treats. There are chocolate-covered pretzels, you know." I point my finger at him. "Normal humans go crazy about that. Not being grateful for a gift is a shitty thing. *And* you'll only regret it when Mrs. Dale down the hall raves about them in the elevator."

He raises his arm above his head and leans against the door frame, giving me quite a vision of the man. "I'm just being what you would expect. The asshole, since I'm a hockey player."

My mouth opens because it feels like he just cut the air,

and instantly I see remorse on his face. He drops his arms and seems to be thinking something.

"Are you mad at me? I'm trying here…" I say softly with so much vulnerability that I feel as though I'm jumping off a cliff.

"I'm sorry. I shouldn't have said that, and I'm not mad at you." He lets out a deep sigh then steps to the side with his hand indicating to come in. "It's just been a tough few days."

Without thought, I accept his invite to enter his home. We stop between the kitchen and living room and face one another.

"I hate mint-flavored bars or any of that puppy chow crap." His eyes drop to the contents that I'm holding. He raises his chin and inspects my hands. "Any brownies in there?"

I break out in a grin and hand him his present. "Of course."

He lifts the lid and makes a sound with a grimace. "Maybe edible."

My hand finds my hip. "Maybe? Geez. Really know how to be grateful."

"Ooh, a Gimel." He sounds pleased.

I rise up on the balls of my feet so I can review what cookie he is holding, and my forehead squinches as he holds a dreidel with something on it. I'm not sure what it means. "You know Hebrew?"

He lifts a shoulder and cooly plays it off. "Long story, but I have a few Jewish relatives, genealogy reports, and the indication that apparently I should have been paying more attention to Hanukkah growing up. Actually, Asher, my coach and cousin-ish, he is half-Jewish. They go hardcore Chrismukkah. So yeah, I can drink your Gimel, Nun, Hey, and Shin under the table."

I stare at him blankly, as I was not expecting that. "Oh, well, that's cool." There is a moment of silence, and I quickly realize why.

His expression turns confused when he pulls out a ginger-bread man, except…

"Is this…?" He holds the cookie up for inspection.

My entire face falls into embarrassment. "I'm going to kill her," I mumble to myself.

"Is this a cookie shaped like a dick?"

My hand comes up to my face to try and cover my flushed warm face that is probably red. "It would appear so, and I'm terribly sorry for… the mix-up." My voice rises an octave.

Now he just smirks at me. "Should I ask why a dick-shaped cookie was even on your cookie-making menu?"

I shake my head feverishly side to side.

He tosses the cookie back as he walks to the counter to set the container down. All the while, I wonder how the knot of the towel hasn't come undone.

The moment he catches me looking at him, I blush and nibble on my bottom lip.

"You okay there?" He is doing his best to maintain his confident smirk.

"Yeah, um, totally." I twist at the bottom of my shirt. "Just wanted to drop them off and apologize. I shouldn't have thrown myself at you."

"No need to apologize, and you didn't throw yourself at me."

Gulping, I'm struggling here because he has swagger when he strides slowly my way.

"Still. You're right to have stopped it and…"

He halts just in front of me, with his body far too close, and I shiver because I can't escape in the best possible way.

His head dips down, and his breath cascades along my cheek until he is near my ear. "Lainey, just because I was a gentleman, doesn't mean I wanted to be one."

I'm about to snap. This overbearing feeling is taking over me. "For the sake of humanity, I need you in more than a towel right now." And ah shit, I just said that out loud.

He retreats his head back slightly, bubbling a deep laugh. "Trust me, answering the door in my towel wasn't on purpose. However, what is it you say? Spread some holiday cheer?"

I sputter out a laugh. "Did you just attempt to be funny?"

The back of his knuckles run along the edge of my jaw while the thumping in my chest is running a marathon, and my core is turning to liquid.

"Since you are having a better day and I have a better understanding of things, can I do something?" He sounds hopeful.

"Is it a better day? You nearly refused my cookies." The corner of his mouth lifts due to my humor, but I turn serious. "Tell me about this something?"

I feel it in my bones. It's the light in his eyes and the tenacity. There is a wave inside of me that roots me down with confidence that all is well.

"You see, I have a little problem."

My eyes drop down. "Is it little?"

"Now who is trying to be funny?"

I clear my throat and put on my serious mode, and he notices. "Okay."

"Even though it wasn't the right circumstance, I haven't been able to stop thinking about something…"

Another step and our bodies are flush.

"Which is?" I rasp.

"This." His mouth crashes down on mine.

Instantly, I'm floating, but I'm in his arms, and he won't let me fall because he's holding me tight. My arms loop around his neck as we kiss gently before returning to our fervent need. I let him lead, otherwise I'm scared I would climb him like a tree, and he's in a towel which is as evil as Krampus, Santa's devilish relative.

I moan into Tyler's mouth, and he only pulls me tighter to his body. My eyes stay closed, and I soak in this moment that is making me lightheaded. This kiss isn't sweet, but it's still perfect because it's filled with reverence. A desperate need for each other.

His tongue runs along the seal of my lips, then he places a simple kiss on the corner of my mouth. But I steal more by chasing his mouth with my own until we mold into another kiss.

It feels like forever, but we need to breathe, and when we do, he slowly pulls away and places a chaste kiss on the tip of my nose and cheek until our foreheads touch, with our breathing rapid, attempting to subside.

"No complaints about your thought process." My voice scrapes with a sultry playful voice. I don't date, and it should scare me, the thought of getting close to a man in a non-platonic way, but no fiber inside of me wants to run away.

"Good."

Pulling away, our eyes meet. We come to terms with what just happened, and we're both radiant because there are no regrets.

"This is the part when I should probably try and save my sanity and not be near you while in a towel and you just kissed me like that," I say flatly, in awe of the last few minutes.

His fingertips touch the curve of my shoulder. "And for

my sanity, I shouldn't be near you while your shoulder is taunting me."

Thank you, Gracie.

It feels as though my lips are swollen, and we both have giddy looks.

"Then I will leave you with a not-nutrition-plan-compliant snack."

"Meh. They can go in the freezer, right?"

I nod.

Walking backward to the front door, our eyes remain tied together. I nearly trip in my step but save myself. My hand lazily indicates behind my back. "I'll just leave then."

"You do that." He grins but also seems flustered himself.

I'm about to dart out but stop. "Hey, Tyler."

"Yeah."

"Maybe you're not like all of the other players."

His lips press together, but the tick of his cheek tells me that he understands.

My chest lifts then eases as I leave his apartment.

Because it seems that he has me feeling a different way than I've experienced before.

CHAPTER 9

TYLER

Leaning against my car after just leaving practice, Charlie is talking my ear off, and it's bitterly cold outside.

He adjusts the strap of his gym bag on his shoulder. "We're doing well," he comments about our last away game and practice today.

"Are you sure the win wasn't some fluke and we got lucky?" I wonder.

He scoffs in annoyance. "You're too hard on yourself. Heaven forbid you actually enjoy a moment worthy of celebration."

My eyes grow wider. "Let's not get too confident. It could be our downfall too. So, no celebrations on my front."

He pinches the tip of his nose, and I can see our breaths in the afternoon sun. "Speaking of festivities, are you going to Bjorn's holiday party?" Charlie asks.

I almost forgot about that. There is not enough time to head back to Sweden for the holidays, which is why he invited the team for a low-key dinner. For anyone who is around, especially those who don't have kids and want to do something. He is doing his best to connect with the team even off the ice. It's hard to be with a team that was left in shambles by the previous coach.

"When the assistant captain puts out an invite like that, kind of need to say yes. Plus, he misses his family back in Sweden. He brought us all of those delicious ginger cookies when it was Saint Lucia's Day. He misses Sweden this time of year," Charlie reminds me with strong pressure for me to go.

"He does live in my building."

"That too. I can't go because we have the holiday show at school, and I already miss enough of my kids' events during the season." It has to be tough for him. Sometimes I believe having kids while playing pro hockey would be too big of a distraction, but these guys still deliver talent on the ice.

Rubbing my hands together, I decide that it is just too freaking cold. "I'll go. Then we have two games and it's Christmas break. Now, I'm heading out. It's too beastly out here to talk."

"Agreed."

We give one another a fist bump, then he heads to his car. Once I'm in mine, I turn off my hockey focus while the engine warms. My mind heads straight to the other night when I kissed Lainey.

I most definitely didn't forget. It's imprinted in every non-hockey thought. Rightfully so, she's a good kisser, and I enjoyed every second. And the coconut bars that was in that magic tin of hers? A fucking bonus to the night.

But now I'm in the situation where I'm back for a few days and I will run into her. What is the next step? There is no possible way to ignore that kiss, and I wouldn't want to. I'm just not sure where it leads us.

I think about this the entire drive home, and all I can

come up with is that it was meant to happen, but do we leave it at that? I'm not sure what she's thinking, but I don't see this as any steps to a future path, only that it's a current step. I'm not blind. She has priorities and so do I. It was fun.

Fun.

Doesn't feel like the right word.

Arriving back at my building, I walk off the elevator, and down the hall, I instantly see a giant box in front of Lainey's.

It has me curious as I approach it, but my attention is broken by the sound of the stairwell door whooshing open.

"Run any faster, will ya?" an exasperated Lainey calls out to Enzo who is bulleting ahead of her.

They must just be getting home from school.

"Hey, Tyler!" Enzo nearly crashes into me as he breaks from his run.

"Someone has energy today," I remark and smile at him.

"We had to make our gifts for our family today at school. It's a candle made from baby food jars," he explains.

Lainey shakes her head as she trails behind him. "I'm not sure I'm supposed to know that."

"But it's the same every year." He doesn't seem to mind his candid response.

For a second my eyes latch with Lainey's, and it's a recognition, as it's clearly on both our minds: the kiss. It's not awkward, and maybe I thought it would be. There is a faint sign of a smile, and still not hidden even with her head wrapped with a beanie on her head and scarf around her neck.

"Whoa, what's this?" An enthusiastic Enzo breaks our fleeting moment because Lainey snaps her sight to the box on the floor.

Instantly, I notice the way she presses her lips together, and her face drops into a cringe. My eyes zip to the box then back to Lainey.

"Can I open it?" Enzo asks, and he's already about to lift the box.

One more swipe of my sight between the box and Lainey. *Ah.*

Santa's delivery.

I place my hand on Enzo's back. "You know what, buddy. They made a mistake. That box is for me. Just boring stuff from sponsors."

"Oh." He frowns.

Lainey mouths a thank-you as Enzo turns, and Lainey quickly hands him the keys. "Homework time." Enzo moans his lack of enthusiasm and slumps his shoulders but listens to his mother.

She cranes her head and peeks through the door to watch him disappear, and when she sees the all-clear, she spins on her feet to face me.

"Thank you. This wasn't supposed to be delivered today."

I have to grin. "Santa?"

She nods and sighs. "Yeah, I did a mass shop of toys and clothes. But they need to be wrapped too."

"Do you have a little elf costume for that?"

She playfully shoves me. "Funny."

Her hand against my chest feels good, and it causes her to pause. She looks at her fingers resting over my coat, and the corner of her mouth twitches. My entire body tightens in the best possible way.

"Uhm." Her thumb begins to swirl because she has no intention of removing her hand. "Can I make a request?"

"Depends. Will we talk about the other night?" I counter.

She forms a bright smile when her eyes flick up. "We probably should do that."

My face eases into a grin. "Fine. What's the request?"

"Can I keep the box at your place?" She uses her head to

indicate her apartment. "Someone is getting relentless in his search for his gifts. Of course, Santa brings the other gifts."

"You want me to hide them?"

She grimaces at her plea. "Even if I still wanted to throttle you, I would ask. I'm getting desperate here."

I chuckle. "So, throttling me is off the table. That's good to know." I answer her request by signaling for her to follow me. I open my door, and she drags the box across the hall. It would be far easier for me to pick it up, but I selfishly enjoy seeing her bent over. It is a view I'm not willing to give up.

She stops her pursuit when the box crosses the threshold of my door, and she leaves it in the front hall. "Is here okay?"

"Yeah, it's fine. I'll move it later." I hang my keys on the hook and slide off my coat.

Then I notice her angelic face and her fingers fidgeting in a cute way. "I guess that means I'll need to come back. Oh, shoot." She snaps her fingers in the air. "What if you are away at a game or practice."

"If you're okay with wrapping after the twenty-third, then I'm home. Otherwise, I'll give you my key."

Her eyes pop out due to the last part of my sentence. Many people give spare sets of keys to neighbors for emergencies. Giving keys to the neighbor that you kissed senseless? Might feel like a different deal.

"Oh. Sure. If you don't mind."

I chuckle to myself. "What is the worst that can happen? You walk in on me in a towel?"

"I mean…" She crosses her arms over her chest. "You could be in no towel."

Stepping closer, I can't let that comment go. "Has me in no towel crossed your mind?" I'm trying to rile her.

She is on to me and rolls her eyes and drops her arms. "Can we switch topics, please?" she implores.

"Fine. But you know what topic we're going to talk about."

She begins to saunter further into my home where the front hall joins the open-plan living room. "We kissed. It happened. That's that." She wants to sound adamant, but she's failing.

In a flash, I grab her arm and reel her into me. "Sure."

The disappointment in her eyes is apparent, but then I feel my sly smirk begin to creep onto my face. "What about this time?" I don't hesitate. My mouth crashes down onto hers, and it's instantly a wildfire.

Is this because I need a release? De-stress from the game season? A little fun? Or because this woman does things to me that are unexplainable.

Truthfully, I know the answer, but right now I don't want to think.

Our kiss turns fast and powerful. Her hair falls behind her shoulders while our lips pressing hard only fuels us more. I can't help myself, and I begin to yank and pull on her scarf that is getting in the way, and her fingers fist my shirt. I seize the opportunity to drag my lips down her neck. Her skin is so damn soft. She chases my mouth to rejoin her for a kiss, and I give in.

But the moment my fingers slide down between us and I fumble with a button, she steps back, creating instant distance.

"Shit." Her hand lands on her forehead.

"What?" Now I'm confused.

"I can't be making out with you. My son is across the hall," she screeches in a whisper.

That does make sense. "Right," I respond simply.

She begins to pace back and forth. "And we did this." She points between us. "Again."

"So. It's a bad thing?" I question as I try to assess her thoughts.

"Not exactly. Maybe unexpected. Or not. I mean, after that kiss the other night, it would kind of be surprising if neither of us wanted a repeat. We seem to be really good at kissing." She reflects during her ramble.

"True." I struggle to contain my laugh at her current state because it's cute and our conversation seems promising.

She looks at me, hopeless, with her cheeks raised from her radiant expression of approval. "What now?"

I shrug. "Not sure."

"It's only a kiss or two—"

"Didn't even need mistletoe." I can't help but make this conversation playful.

She stops mid-pace to give me a hardened look. "Well, kissing is kissing. It's not like we slept together."

I tut. "That *would* require mistletoe." Why am I teasing her so much? In most cases, I would probably be an ass right now. However, there haven't really been times when there is a woman in front of me who I have respect for and want to kiss her all over again.

"Cute," she replies dryly.

I completely ease into a smile. "I'm not sure what you want me to do right now."

She snickers a sound then beams her hopelessness with a smile. "Neither of us know. And right now, I need to get back to Enzo."

"Of course." I'm serious. Scratching the back of my neck, I stand on the side as she directs herself back to my front door.

For reasons beyond me, an idea comes to me. A risky one, but I can't seem to bury it.

"Lainey, how do you feel about holiday parties?" She

stares at me blankly, unsure of why I asked that. "I have to go to one that Bjorn invited the guys to, if you want to come along."

She seems taken aback by my invitation and ponders my question for a few ticks.

Her entire body relaxes, and her smile reappears. "He invited one of your neighbors who has a brother who plays hockey, too." She raises her hand a little. "Plus, I love holiday parties. Gingerbread houses, latkes, and I heard Bjorn normally even gives out Swedish candy in little stockings. What's not to love?"

Swiping the back of my finger across my jaw, I have to smile wryly. "I should have guessed you would say that. But I mean, going to the party… with me."

"Yeah. I understood that part of your question, but the overbearing reminder of a completely different holiday menu overcame me." Now she's just straight-up flirtatious with me. "But yeah, the joining-you part I got. And… I love holiday parties even better when I get to sit on Santa's lap." She winks to rile me up.

I guess I have a date.

CHAPTER 10
LAINEY

What am I doing?

I pace by the front door, waiting for a knock. My black dress with a small glitter pattern clings to my body but not in a too-much-skin kind of way. Why did I agree to this?

Enzo is at a sleepover, and I haven't dated in a long time. This isn't exactly a date, is it? I'm doing him a favor. A big one, because the idea of standing in a party full of hockey guys isn't exactly up there on my list of holiday wishes. But Bjorn has always been kind and respectful when my brother was around. However, when Tyler asked me to join, maybe this caused my blood pressure to spike a bit, and it wasn't half bad. Maybe it's time to get out of my comfort zone.

The knock on my door stops me in my tracks, and my eyes drill into the back of the door as if it will suddenly burst into flames. It's nerves. That explains the butterflies letting loose inside of me.

After a calm reassuring breath and rolling my shoulders back, I decide I can do this. I open the door, and Tyler is standing there with a cocky grin already painted on his face.

His hair is slightly gelled back, causing his eye color to intensify, and his blazer with dress shirt and dark jeans is formal enough but shows his laidback, albeit sometimes uptight personality. He has a clearly expensive bottle of wine in his hand, too.

"Hi." Maybe he can hear my nerves.

His eyes roam all over me, and without any words leaving his mouth, I'm getting concerned. "Is everything okay?"

"Yeah, it's just the dress."

Now I'm examining myself and drop my gaze down to check my body. "Oh, is it too much? I guess I can go change."

His hand darts out to touch my arm and ease me. "No, no, it's not that. It's perfect on you. You're beautiful. I'm kind of scared that I'll be warning the rookies to stay on the other side of the room."

My smile spreads because a compliment is a compliment.

Then we both seem to stall. I notice that his eyes squinch together, and I feel self-conscious.

"What?" My brows knit together.

His smile is almost wistful. "There's glitter on your hand."

My eyes plunge down, and the corner of my mouth snags. "Hazards of my job. Preschoolers and glitter that never wants to come off. It's holiday season, which means every day there is a new craft and holiday. Today was decorating your own dreidel for Hanukkah."

The back of his knuckle scrapes along his stubbled jaw. "It suits you at least. Matches your eyes."

"Don't try to charm me through cheesy lines."

"I would never. Ready to go?"

"Yeah. It will take us forever to get there," I tease. "You know, traffic on the stairs and all."

I twist my body to reach behind me for my sweater on the hook by the door. To my surprise, he takes my sweater and opens it to help me slip it on. Lines form on my forehead as I pick up my own bottle of wine from the side table. A gift is a gift no matter if the bottle was on sale.

"Not going to lie. Gentleman Tyler is kind of discerning. I'm not used to this."

He chuckles once. "I can be full of surprises. Just like, we will be wearing Santa hats." On cue, he pulls them out of his back pocket. "Asher issued a memo that the team should have a little more positive holiday cheer."

"He said it like that?"

"No. But then marketing told us that we need to get it together because our pre-game arrival photos are not up to par with other teams'. When one of the guys said he has an elf hat and another guy said reindeer ears, I opted for Santa. It's sophisticated enough if I had to choose from those options."

The way this guy thinks puts a smile on my face.

It's when we begin to walk down the stairs that I become positive that this is going to be a night to remember.

I'M grateful when the group at Bjorn's isn't too big or small. The apartment is beautiful, with garland and white lights all around. I also appreciate that Tyler introduced me to some of the new players as his neighbor. Many already know that I'm Seb's little sister, but there have been a lot of trades lately, though a few faces are the same.

For a millisecond, my mind sends a signal to my body that I would probably be disappointed if Tyler got traded.

Tyler's hand is on my back as we stand with drinks in

hand, listening to Bjorn. He is telling us about how his parents are going to fly in and stay a few weeks later in the season. He's superstitious and believes having his mom at a game will bring extra luck.

"I hope one day my son thinks that way," I quip before taking a sip of my wine.

"He will. Enzo is crazy about you," Tyler assures me.

Bjorn smiles as his eyes swim between Tyler and me. "When will he start playing hockey?"

The question on everyone's mind when it comes to Seb's nephew. "Believe it or not, I'm not so great on skates. Seb was in charge of Enzo when it came to anything hockey. But until the season breaks, Enzo is just going to have to wait."

"Nah, I can take him," Tyler offers.

My eyes swing to him. He says it so casually, and that's what surprises me. I should be fighting the idea that he could be a male figure in Enzo's life, because it's dangerous. Enzo needs stability. However, everything inside of me reassures me that all is well.

"Want another drink?" he asks because he has no clue the current status of my brain.

"Sure," I nimbly reply.

I can't help it, but my eyes follow Tyler working his way through the crowd of people.

"He's a good guy," Bjorn mentions. "Strong ethic out there on the ice, and off the ice, he's kind of quiet. Actually, a bit reserved at times, but every team has one of those guys. You're close with him?"

My lashes flutter because I take a moment. "We're just neighbors." I shrug.

He curls his lip and makes a noise as his head tips gently to the side. "He kind of has this… what's the word…" It's obvious that he's searching in his head, which is fair enough, as English isn't his first language, then he snaps his fingers. "Aura. That's it."

I scoff a laugh. "That would be because Scrooge is in the midst of holiday season."

"What I meant is lately he's been… He actually smiles… voluntarily," he simply states.

Is it because of me?

"Must be because of the garland above his door or something." I quickly pretend to take a sip of my empty glass as my eyes scan around the room in an attempt to avoid any further details.

I'm thankful when Tyler reappears with a drink for me. "What have you two been talking about?" He hands me a new small glass, and I set the old one down on a nearby table.

"You." Bjorn stares at him seriously, only to break out in a wide grin a few seconds later. "You look good in a Santa hat. It will help you when we break out some games later. Someone's girlfriend mentioned Who Am I or whatever the hell that game is." Bjorn pats Tyler's back in passing.

Tyler stands in front of me with a subtle wry smile. "Should I be worried?"

I laugh once. "You're fine."

"They were handing these out in the kitchen." He holds up his small glass of clear liquid.

Glancing down at my own, I shrug and decide to give it a try, only to nearly spit it out. "Whoa. What is this?" It's enough alcohol for the entire year.

"Some kind of schnapps or something. I'm not sure, but it tastes kind of lethal."

"*Yeah*, I'm gonna go easy on this one."

He chuckles, and his brows rise as he quickly clinks my shot glass then downs his as if he is a pro. He smiles at me.

"What? He made the team drink this at the end of last season. It's not my first rodeo."

"I noticed."

For the next hour, we each get caught in conversations with others. Tyler is busy talking to teammates but appears to be relaxed, and I only hear various tail ends of his conversations but there isn't much hockey talk. Meanwhile, I catch up with girlfriends of a few of the guys that I already knew.

It's getting late or at least for my standards. Quickly I go to the restroom and emerge only to nearly run into Tyler.

"There you are."

I stare at him strangely. "Scared I ditched you?" I tease.

He lifts a shoulder, and I wonder if he is buzzed, but he doesn't appear to be. Maybe a little loose from a drink or two but definitely completely aware of the way his eyes are spearing into me, and my body is beginning to quicken.

"I like the necklace." He steps forward, and his hooked finger glides along a strand of gold garland wrapped around my neck because I added it half an hour ago when someone wanted to swap for my hat. The way his eyes drop down to where he is touching me below my collarbone, it's as though his finger is a feather dancing around my chest.

I step closer to him, feeling a wave of sensuality flood me. There is nobody around, but it still feels dangerous. "Sorry, I decided being Santa's helper isn't for me," I softly inform him, and I notice how my voice is flirty.

His eyes meet mine, and for a second of silence, it's clear what we both want to suggest.

"We've made an appearance, and they're setting up for karaoke which is my sign that we should escape."

"I couldn't agree more," I insist.

His lips purse as he blows out an audible exhale, as

though he needs to cool himself off. He must be heating up the way I am.

It's a quick goodbye and thank-you to Bjorn. I'm happy he is enjoying himself tonight, plus it was super sweet that he sent us home with *knack*, a sort of Swedish toffee for Enzo.

Arriving in front of our doors, we both stall. My eyes look everywhere except at Tyler. Everything inside of me is racing.

"Well, that was fun. He's a good guy," I attempt to make conversation.

"Yep." Tyler taps his foot on the carpet, and I'm about to say something, but he beats me to it. "Listen, about that kiss…"

I'm going to go bold, and I ensure that our eyes lock together. "Can we just admit that we both want this night to end only one way?"

His entire body deflates as though he was holding air in. "Thank fuck."

Tyler storms to me, and his lips crash onto mine, and in unison, his hand fists my hair by my back.

I almost fall down, but he pulls me to him to ensure I regain my balance.

"Your place or mine?" His breath is already labored, which is fair enough because the man's kisses should be criminal.

No hesitation from me, I walk him back. "Yours. There are blocks everywhere at my place, and we can't afford an injury from stepping on the walk of death." It might sound humorous but I'm serious as can be.

I drape my arms around his shoulders, causing him to fumble with his keys, as he is in a rush. "Your stupid garland is getting tangled around my arm." With frustration, he rips the tinsel off my body and carelessly throws it onto the ground before opening the door with gusto.

We nearly tumble into his place, and he kicks the door behind him closed. Already halfway down the hall, we are pawing one another in an effort to get clothes off. It all happens so fast that I'm not sure when he managed to peel off his shirt. The moment we are in his room, he turns me around and searches for the zip on my dress. I lift my hair to the side, and he unzips me roughly, and I hear a snap.

"Broke the zip. I'll get you a new dress," he promises matter-of-factly before he spins me around and yanks me against his body.

We seal our mouths together, and our middles mold together, warm skin against warm skin.

A slow shiver moves down my spine because his heat radiates against my skin. I like us this close. It's the excitement that I've been anticipating all night. My breath catches as his fingers move painfully slowly along the curve of my body as he removes the dress. It is a light touch, but it is powerful enough.

The fabric falls to the floor, and I slowly peer up at him, still in my bra and panties. His eyes skate up and down my body, and the corner of his mouth hitches up. "Beautiful."

I'm too confident to blush. It might have been a while but I'm not nervous. Especially with the way he looks at me. "So what do we do now?" My voice is sultry but playful.

His arm wraps around my middle, bringing me flush against his body.

"We don't stop," he replies directly.

"Good answer."

He falls back onto the bed, taking me with him, and I can't help but giggle as I roll to my side. "Uh, you still have your pants on. Not fair on the clothing quota." My hands trail beneath his bellybutton, feathery with my touch.

"Something tells me that you will find a solution to that." He assists me in the pursuit to unbuckle his pants.

I can't help it, and I pause when I see his half-naked body; biting my lip, I take in the view. "You're a crime to humanity."

He zips down and pulls the denim aside. "Wait until you see what else is in store."

Kicking his jeans off, he is quick to hover over me, and I can't help but notice his eyes have a primal need. A wicked smirk is faint on his face. I don't get to admire him for long, as his lips crash against mine.

Until this moment, we've been in a rush, a crazed pursuit to give in to the tension that has surrounded us for a long time. We slow down, and it only magnifies this moment. Maybe we both realize we don't need to hurry, which sets my body on fire.

Our eyes search, and I can only describe it as recognition to what we are doing.

The gentle kiss on my lips sends me into a sinking feeling only made more intense as his mouth travels down my neck, leaving a warm path, and I can't control the needy sound leaving me.

My hips rise because I need more contact from him. There is a wave of heat running through me that is desperate for more. I'm aching between my legs. Gosh, I could drown in the smell of his cologne; it's not too strong, but it tingles my nose.

"I want to kiss every part of this body," he murmurs against my skin.

I croon when his mouth covers the thin lace fabric over my hard nipple.

"No complaints from me," I breathe. I comb my fingers through his hair because I need to grip something. And even though I feel his hard cock under his boxer briefs, I can't help it; my fingers continue to rake down his body, my nails probably leaving marks on his back, but I can't control it, as I'm so far on a mission for more that the thought of creating distance seems far too hollow.

The moment that I manage to grab his boxers' waistband, his sinister throaty chuckle fills the room, and his mouth brushes down my stomach in unison with his body slithering down. He's made it impossible for me to put in effort to remove my bra.

"My way," he whispers in warning, adjusting his body, causing my thighs to open, and he lies on his stomach.

My entire body trembles in anticipation because his mouth feathers my skin near my hip bone.

"Fuck." I tighten my lips together because I have an idea of what he is about to do.

"I'll start with my tongue. Then, if you are a good girl, I will give you more."

I hum a response that isn't one at all. It's my body becoming molten, and I'm unable to speak.

The moment his mouth covers the thin, soaked fabric between my legs, I moan. My clit is desperate for relief, and it's barely relieved when the tip of his nose hits that little spot while his tongue swipes up my slit. The indescribable sound he makes is a moan because he's enjoying this as much as I am.

"Tyler," I plead.

The only response I get is his hands holding my hips down to enable his teeth to nip the fabric.

His sight glides up, and with purpose, his tongue darts out and circles my clit. I watch, and my pulse accelerates.

Everything inside of me is on fire, straight down to my toes.

He hesitates, maybe waiting for my cue, so I nod once. He slips his fingers under my panties and pulls them down. Scooting up onto his knees, he drags the fabric as he raises my legs.

"All of it off, Lainey." He taunts his demand.

Sitting up slightly, I reach behind my back to unclasp my bra. He abandons me the moment my good-as-gone lace underwear is on the floor. I hear the sound of the drawer on the nightstand open, and he returns with a condom.

The view of him throwing his boxer briefs to the side ups the ante, and more heat pools below my belly. My eyes grow into saucers because his cock is long and girthy.

"Like what you see?" That cocky grin is my undoing.

I'm far too eager for him to hurry up. "I give credit where credit is due."

The sound of the wrapper opening only excited me. I'm doing this… with him. Never would have thought, but apparently somewhere deep in my mind there has always been a wild dream for him.

His hungry eyes lock with mine as his knee dips into the mattress, and I return to my back. I can't help it, and I reach out to his hips to encourage him to take me.

My thighs part, and he moves into position. "No going back after this, Lainey. But you are too drenched that I have an idea of what your answer might be."

My clit throbs because I'm desperate to unravel. "Please," I beg.

The devilish smirk is back, and my eyes close the moment his cock slides between my folds, feeling how wet I am.

"Look at me." Tyler is direct, and my eyes fly open.

He begins to enter me slowly, controlled, deeper, and then

some more. He groans as he pulls back, then drives right back in.

I squeeze my core and breathe heavily, his rhythm only leading me closer to relief.

"Fuck," he curses to himself. His arms hook under my knees, and he splays me wide as he speeds up.

My fingers claw into the mattress, and our eyes meeting only intensifies this moment.

We stay in the pattern until finally, my body explodes from my orgasm that's been dying to escape. He stays inside me as I shake, and he is relentless in the pursuit of his orgasm.

"You look fucking good when you come around my cock." His rugged breathy voice drips with satisfaction. He pushes into me only to slide out, then back in with abandon. He uses me the way he needs until he follows with his own release.

He stills inside me before he falls onto the bed, completely spent. I feel my own pounding chest and his is visibly moving.

"Give me a sec," he breathes out and rolls out of bed.

I pull the duvet to me and stare at the ceiling as my heartrate settles. Smiling to myself, I'm really liking the way this evening turned out. I take a moment to observe my surroundings because admittedly, I kind of skipped that part when we were in our clawing-clothes-off hysteria.

Huh, so this is where Tyler sleeps.

The door to his walk-in closet is slightly ajar but all I see is a line of suits. Admittedly, I might have joined half the female population stopping mid-scroll when the team posts pre-game photos. A guy in a hockey uniform is okay, but a hockey guy in a suit is a full-on eleven out of ten.

"What has you smiling?"

I sit up partly on my propped elbows. "Nothing crazy."

He slides under the covers to join me. Only for a second do I remember that leaving or him wanting me to go could be an option. However, he seems intent on having me stay.

"I hope you don't hog the sheets."

On purpose, I tug the duvet from his side of the bed. "I would never."

He rolls to his side to mirror my position. He reclaims his sheets with one jerk. "Equal distribution."

"Fair enough."

"What are the chances since we are sharing a bed that I get to fuck you again before morning?"

"Very high."

The tips of his fingers begin to caress my upper arm, and I rest the side of my face on my hand on the pillow.

"I'm not entirely sure I'll feel my legs tomorrow," I admit.

"I have a foam roller that I use for my muscles if that will help," he jokes.

I smile because we always seem to channel one another's humor. In fact, we are often attuned to when we should quarrel and when to be funny.

We take a solid minute to study one another's bodies. I trace my fingers over the muscles on his chest, and it's not a myth that athletes are toned.

His mouth opens to speak. "Tell me, other than your holiday cheer and fucking me, what are your hobbies?"

"Oh, I…"

"You're a great mom, so don't tell me it's whatever Enzo wants to do."

My eyes grow because the guy is observant. "I don't doubt I'm a good mom, but a seven-year-old takes a lot of energy, and he always wants to try new things. I would say baking is my thing. I can do it with him or by myself."

"I've eaten half of the tin that I put in my freezer. Kind of addictive."

He grabs my leg to splay across his waist. My hips press into his thigh because my clit needs friction, but the sheet between us is an obstacle that we don't need. "Uh-oh, what will you do to me?"

"My favorite hobby."

"Which is…"

His chuckle is sinister, and it sends vibrations straight to my pussy. "Licking you right before I fuck you as deep as possible."

My thighs part open, and I bite my bottom lip to keep me from being too needy. "That…" I coo a sound because I have zero restraint. "I'm on board with that."

His cock is already at full attention. My palm grips around the base of his cock, and the sound of Tyler moaning pleases me.

"Fuck," he hisses.

Wrapping my lips around the tip of his cock, I swirl my tongue. I wouldn't say that I'm talented in this department or that I have much experience, but I want to try. Taking more of him in my mouth, I continue to lick and suck. Tyler drops his hand down to brush my hair away from my face, and if affection and a blowjob entwine together, then that is this moment. Because his fingers gently hold my head to guide me.

He moans, and it encourages me even more. I take a breath, but my hand continues to pump him. My mouth is salivating, and filling it with his cock is the only answer, otherwise my chin will be a mess.

Taking him deeper, I'm wet between my thighs because

this turns me on. I speed up, but he takes my hand and leads me off his cock.

"I'm enjoying this, but let me fuck that pussy of yours." He drops my hair and reaches for the drawer, and I coast up his body. "On top of me," he directs.

Straddling him, I instantly make the skin on his upper thigh a mess with my arousal. The moment that the condom is on, I align myself, and he frames my body with his hands, aiding my direction as I root down on his cock.

We both breathe out loud, and the way he stares up at me is pure desire. What man wouldn't want a naked woman on top of him? Except, this isn't that. I don't know his history, only that he is pretty tame on the dating front compared to other guys on the team. But in this moment, it seems as though I'm a woman that he has been saving time for.

This angle is far more intense than I imagined. His cock hits deep and hard, and my body sinks down on him which only fills me up to the point I'm tight around him.

"You okay?"

My nostrils flare from my sharp breath. "Yes, it feels really good, but… wow, you are big."

He grins to himself. My admittance must be a signal for him because he uses his strength to flip us, and the moment he re-enters me, I appreciate how he seems to read my body.

It's also scary because how can that be? This is our first night together.

First… it would imply that there may be a second.

It doesn't matter because the way our bodies frame together, I don't want to settle for one night only.

The thought floating in my head mixed with my oversensitive body relaxes me for the next few minutes before he brings my orgasm to a near roar. I clench his cock and grip his arms to hang on while I shake. It brings on his own orgasm, chasing my own.

We slow together as we both come down from the high we created. My heart is racing and his labored breath and the view of his chest moving confirms his body is experiencing the same need to recover from the explosion we just created.

I'm dizzy from how good the last hour has made me physically feel.

For now, we need a little rest. I snuggle into the mattress and adjust the sheets and duvet. It's time to sleep.

"Are you thinking what I'm thinking?" Tyler gives me a knowing look as he adjusts his pillow.

"I think so."

"Sleep," we say in unison.

We both scoot into the middle, my eyes already heavy and ready to close. His arm loops around me to pull me close against his body.

"I forgot to ask if you want a shirt to sleep in?"

"It's okay. I'm fine."

"Good answer."

We both stop squirming and find our embrace for rest.

With my eyes closed, I hum a sound. "It's nice to fall asleep tired not due to motherhood. Now it's all because of you, and I'm not complaining."

He snickers a sound of approval in response and pulls me closer. "Sleep, Lainey. We still have the morning."

Sighing, I feel my slumber take over, with the ease of feeling and believing that tonight was a special night.

CHAPTER 11
TYLER

Lying on my side, I rest my head against my propped elbow while I watch Lainey sleep. The sheet is where it should be, haphazardly wrapped around her naked body. The morning light streaming through my large windows somehow indicates a cold day ahead.

I need to wake her, and as much as it's because of my morning wood, I remember she mentioned having to pick up Enzo this morning. The back of my knuckle feathers a few strokes along the length of her arm, and her body begins to stir.

"Lainey," I whisper.

"Hmm." She sounds groggy and tries to pull the sheet up under her chin, but I'll have none of that, and I yank it down.

"Wakey, wakey."

She begins to squint her eyes until they are fully open. "What time is it?" Lainey is still in her sleepy daze.

I sit up and glance at the clock on the side table. "Eight."

Slowly, she sits up. "Okay. I should probably get going." She rubs the side of her head while she yawns.

I'm kind of amused, as I'm waiting for something.

She seems to be more awake, and her hand plops down on the mattress. She looks down then up before her eyes swing side to side. "Oh yeah. I'm here."

I sputter a laugh. "You forgot?"

It causes her lips to curve up into a soft smile. "No. I'm just not… wait. What? I mean, we slept together and got something out of our systems…"

I throw her a brazen look. "Want me to kick you out at the speed of light?" I tease.

She finds my antics humorous enough. "Well, it's been fun." She swings her legs to the edge of the bed and drags the blankets with her.

Okay, she's leaving? Meaningless sex, right?

When she stands, she has a sly smirk on her mouth when she glances over her shoulder at me. "Gotcha." She's joking with me.

Getting out of bed while shaking my head, I walk to my dresser to find a pair of sweatpants, meanwhile Lainey gives up on trying to fix the zipper I broke on the side of her dress.

"Want a coffee?"

"Tempting, but I actually need to go shower, change, and pick up Enzo at 10."

"You could shower here if you want," I offer.

She wiggles her finger side to side. "Nuh-uh. I'll never leave then."

A cocky grin hits me instantly. "Ah, so I *am* good."

Lainey bites her smile. "I mean, not bad."

Rolling my shirt down over my body, I dangerously meet her eyes, and her little joke just won't do this morning. "Guess I'll have to try harder next time."

Her breath gets caught somewhere inside of her. "Next time." I can barely hear her, but I do. "So, there will be another time?" She sounds doubtful.

Taking another step closer to her, I refrain from shaking her because she already knows the answer. "Why not?"

"I guess we know what this is." Her bottom lip is trapped between her teeth.

My hands land on her shoulders, and I direct her to turn. "Exactly." Walking behind her, I lead her straight to my kitchen. "You don't need to run away if that was actually what you were doing. Remember, I have decent coffee."

"Okay, okay. You win."

"I always win." I'm not sure my vigor of an answer is about this or my natural hockey talk.

She giggles, either way.

My hands vacate her shoulders when we are in the middle of the kitchen, and I begin to think about the coffee machine but stop and catch her off guard with a kiss. One where she loses her balance, but I wrap my arms around her.

Fuck morning breath. We both had enough candy canes last night to keep our breath fresh until New Year's. That means we don't need to delay a morning kiss.

But we escalate, and next thing I know her hand sneaks between us and heads down to the waistband of my sweats because I've been hard since 0.02 seconds after kissing her, and her body is pressed against mine.

Our noses touch and our mouths part. Our breathing is heavy, and the urge to rush into throwing her over my shoulder and carrying her back to my bedroom runs strong.

However, I've been on Santa's naughty list, which is why fate decided that my cell should start vibrating on my counter where I left it on the charger overnight.

I groan, but I feel Lainey smile against my mouth. "Go." She pushes me slightly away.

"Not cool."

Walking to my phone, I see the name on the screen as

clear as day, and I know that my mom will not relent. It will be a call, voicemail, text, then another try in about an hour.

I grumble a noise and bring the phone to my ear. "Yes?" I dryly greet her as I stare at Lainey.

"Ho-ho-ho to you too." My mother is too cheery for me at this time of the morning.

Lainey must hear because she stifles a laugh.

"What is it?"

"Great news. Your guest room is going to be put to good use."

Dread. Absolute dread fills me.

"Yep. We are coming for Christmas. You're welcome. No need to work on our invitation." I can hear it in her voice that she is smiling and she is sarcastic today, *lovely*.

I pinch the bridge of my nose and digest the news. Being a big boy and staying firm that my guest room is off limits is hard when your parents are good people and have only ever supported you. Most of my friends have always said my parents are fun, and I happen to understand their views.

"Okay," I agree tightly to becoming a host with definitely not the mostest.

"Perfect. You have the tree and decorations, right?"

"Is that really needed?" I press.

She laughs, and Lainey smiles with her. These two women don't even need to meet; they are both throwing my morning off.

"Of course. If we are going to have a proper Christmas Day, then at least put in a little effort," she chides.

I bite down my protest. "Guess I'll find a tree," I grind out in response.

"Wonderful." Her peppiness is back in full swing. "One more thing…"

"Yes?"

"Your Aunt Harper and Uncle Max are visiting Illinois since your cousins are with their respective in-laws, and they will be staying in a hotel near you. They managed to get the last room. So please plan accordingly to host us all during the day."

My jaw goes slack as I take a few beats to adjust to the new situation. "Are you kidding me? We're adding Hanukkah to the day too?"

Lainey's eyes grow big, and her beaming smile hasn't changed.

"You know how she gets. Over the top is the only way, so yes, menorah, dreidels, not a morsel of pig even if it's candy-shaped. Just do vegetarian. Make it happen."

"Two years ago, she made the entire family go on a gelt scavenger hunt." My voice rises.

"Cute, huh?" My mom is oblivious.

"It lasted three hours!"

"Only because it turned into a drinking game," she defends.

Shaking my head, I feel the need to point out, "And Passover? Should I not remind you of the year that went down in the history books."

"Hey, it is not my fault that we are required to drink four glasses of wine… and I thought it was grape juice. That stuff almost tastes the same, and it is damn good," she snaps in her defense before calming. "I'll call you later. I'm going to check the bakery here for what I might be able to order and bring with us. Love you." She hangs up before I can absorb any more details.

My hand with my phone drops to my side, and I look at the floor as I come to terms with the change of events. But my eyes quickly draw up when Lainey bursts out laughing.

"This isn't funny."

Her hand flies up as she tries to calm her hysterics, but it is an easy fail. "I'm sorry, but it is." She plants her hands on her stomach as she continues. I just watch, not amused in the slightest.

Finally, she grasps my demeanor and swallows a laugh and then attempts to keep back another. "What?" A chuckle escapes. "But this *is* hilarious."

I stomp to my coffee machine and begin to work on my cup of coffee with blunt movements.

Lainey walks behind me, and her lone finger scratches my upper back before crawling to my shoulder and urging me to turn and face her. Her face is subdued, but she is still fighting a grin.

"I remember you mentioned the Jewish family factor."

I shake my head. "Yeah, well, my aunt converted when she met her husband. She had one of those crazy mothers-in-law who taught her to cook and traditions. It has equated to my aunt acting batshit crazy on holidays that involve food, alcohol, and games. That basically describes every Jewish holiday on the calendar. News flash, there are a lot of holidays. Then it was discovered when someone in the family did one of those genealogy test things that apparently our grandmother's second cousin of another cousin, I lost track who, is Jewish on our side of the family, and imagine how that upped my aunt's crazy."

Lainey shrugs. "I get it. Gracie has a similar background. Her mom is Jewish and dad not. But just order a menorah online. It will probably get here by tomorrow. The big store off the highway is sold out. They were next to the Hanukkah gift bags that were squeezed between Kwanzaa and the snowmen-themed decorations. I had to look for school, we needed a few supplies."

My fingers comb through my hair. "And a fucking tree?

What should I do about that? I will get the third degree if it isn't a real tree. My parents are all about aesthetic and visuals since that's their career."

She squares my shoulders to her. "No biggie. You are off now, and they arrive, what? Tomorrow night?" I nod. "You have plenty of time to get a tree. I know where."

"Then what?" My voice rises an octave.

"You need to decorate," she deadpans and looks at me as if I'm a moron.

My response is to sigh heavily. The smile painted on her lips is a tad comforting.

"I have to pick up Enzo, but we can go with you. It might go faster because I have a strange feeling that you don't know what you are looking for." Her face screws up.

"No shit."

Her smile wobbles because she wants to laugh again, I know she does. "You can do this." Excitement begins to spread all over her face. "It's been fun." She points between us. "But I've gotta run. I fucked like crazy last night and now I need to help the guy find a tree. What a random hookup experience."

All I manage is a few scratchy sounds that escape from my throat when she winks at me before skipping away, giving me zero chance to tell her to stop and let us have sex to cure my distraught state.

CHAPTER 12
TYLER

My head tilts in different angles as I stare skeptically at the tree that Enzo shows me at Olive Owl, a winery a few towns over owned by the Blisswood family.

I review the tree under the afternoon daylight. "I mean, it has bones." Which equates to missing a lot of branches.

Lainey elbows my arm as she stands by my side. "Fewer pine needles on the floor," she points out positively.

"It's a little colorful," I add. That equates to brown.

"It'll match your light choices."

"What would that be?" I'm clueless.

She playfully swats my shoulder. "White, silly. It's classic."

"It's the right height." One thing that's true. It's taller than me.

"How are we going to get this tree home?" Enzo continues to look at his tree choice, and I don't have the heart to tell him that he needs to improve on this skill.

"Luckily, I have a state-of-the-art car and a roof that is suitable to drive this baby home."

Enzo snickers. "If you say so. It's cold. Can we get hot apple cider while we're here?"

Lainey leans down and rewraps the scarf around his neck. "Depends if Scrooge here will allow us a break. He has a long list of things to do, so he's working us to the bone."

"Boney like the tree," I quip to myself. Lainey spears me with her gaze. She wants me to be a little more positive today. Smile a little more too. "Yeah, of course, cider is on me."

"And the cookies shaped like trees?" Enzo adds to his list.

"Yes."

His toothy grin causes a crack of a smile on my face. "I'll pay for the tree and have someone help me with my car. Will you get me an eggnog?"

Lainey's eyes grow to saucers because she's surprised by my choice of a holiday-themed drink.

"I've heard their recipe has rum," I highlight mundanely.

She laughs because she catches on that I am joking then walks with Enzo toward the main farmhouse.

Fifteen minutes later, we are all set, and I join Lainey and Enzo inside. They managed to grab a table in the corner. There is something kind of cozy about a fireplace warming the room and green garland wrapped around the space. A fire hazard, but fine.

"What's the latest on your search?" Lainey inquires as I scroll on my phone.

"No luck. If I wanted guaranteed delivery for a menorah then I shouldn't have waited until Hanukkah is already in full swing." I raise my finger in the air. "Oh yeah, I didn't wait, instead my crazy family decided to spring this on me at the last minute."

"We had to learn the Hanukkah song at school," Enzo mentions as he digs his spoon into the whipped cream on the hot chocolate he opted for instead of cider.

"I vaguely remember learning it in school. *Oh Hanukkah, Oh Hanukkah.*"

Lainey squeezes my arm from where she sits by my side. "Look at you. Maybe your family will request karaoke hour as well." She smiles cheekily.

Glaring at her, I only kind of—okay, I do find her whole attitude cute. "Laugh all you want, but you don't know my aunt. I'll never hear the end of this."

She seems sympathetic. "We'll figure it out."

I love the way she says *we*.

We've been so busy all day that I haven't thought once about what is transpiring between us. Mostly because… every moment that we experience now is too easy and natural. Nothing inside of me seems to be freaking out about her. That honor is reserved for my family.

"Do you get extra presents? Laura at school is guaranteed eight presents," Enzo says with his mouth full of a whipped cream.

"No. My parents celebrate Christmas. But sometimes we have eccentric relatives that decide that merging two holidays together is bigger than winning a hockey cup." Lainey has a closed-mouth smile because maybe I need to work on my deliverance of not-so-festive cheer. I'll try again. "I mean, it does end up with some pretty epic dinners."

"Tomorrow, we're going to stop by a friend's who I work with. She invited us for breakfast. Gracie canceled breakfast because of some family situation or something. Probably had to swap mornings that she sees her half-brother."

That reminds me of something. "Yeah? Strange thing. She was at the rink talking to Asher."

"Really?" She seems surprised then shrugs. "I'll ask her next time I see her. Anyhow, we also call the family and collapse on the couch in our pajamas. Basically, the sequel to

Thanksgiving," Lainey explains then blows on the mug between her hands.

"Except there are presents," Enzo reminds us.

"Depends. Has the magical elf been reporting to Santa every night that you are the perfect little angel?" Lainey is a great mom. She makes everything look effortless.

"Of course, and we're going to leave out his favorite cookies this year." This kid is so damn excited.

Lainey glances sidelong at me. "Have you heard through the grapevine what Santa's favorite cookies are this year?" She wants me to join in on her theatrics.

"Probably those wafer things."

"Really?" Her face squinches from my choice.

But I'm messing with her. "Nah, he's a classic chocolate chip kind of guy. Maybe this year with those red and green chocolates in the cookies."

"I've heard that too," she agrees.

"We have to get that, Mom."

I motion to the waitress that I'm going to pay. "Good thing we have to run to the store. We need lights."

Because my day of decorating misery is never-ending. Except… I'm kind of enjoying this.

THE TREE in front of my big bay window in my living room is doable. It does need a little help, but I guess that's what the decorations are for. After scavenging the store's shelves for the last of the holiday decorations, we managed to find some things, and we came home. Lainey and Enzo needed to call her brother, and she wanted to do a few things around the house.

When the knock on the door finally comes, I'm relieved.

Answering, Lainey is smiling brightly as she holds a craft out in front of her.

"Solved," she says proudly.

I study it, and instantly I smile.

It's a menorah.

Stepping aside, Lainey enters my place. "Enzo has crashed. He is just going to chill on the couch with a movie, but he made this for you."

Accepting the gift from her hand, it's definitely from a kid, but it's pretty darn cool.

He used foil to create candle sticks and popsicle sticks to create the base. Most of all, he made it for me because he likes me, and that matters.

"It's great." I'm being honest.

She claps her hands together. "Perfect. Now on to your tree."

I can't help but stay put and watch her eagerly head straight to the branches and kneel down to unpack the shopping bags.

I hate it.

That her mood is becoming infectious, and I like her a little more during the holiday season. It freaks me out that I might actually have a spot inside of me that isn't focused on hockey.

After ogling her a little longer, I come to her aide.

"I follow you, boss," I inform her.

She is already ripping open a box of tree lights. "First lights, then ornaments, and maybe I have some more sparkly garland in a box somewhere."

"Let's just stick to what is right in front of us," I suggest.

She stalls for a moment, and our eyes lock. Probably because there are interpretations for that sentence, and it has nothing to do with decorations.

What is happening?

Her lips pinch, and she seems to reflect for a moment. "Okay, you take one side of the tree, and I'll take the other. We need to weave the lights."

"Sure."

She begins on the other side of the tree near the base. "I'll pass it to you, then you hang lights then pass back to me and so on."

"Got it. It's not rocket science," I assure her and stand in my spot.

"I can't believe this is happening. Mr. Grump has no choice but to celebrate Chrismukkah. Two great holidays rolled into one." She's elated as she strings the lights along, and then I take over.

"Okay, we established you have received your bonus gift of the year of my holiday demise."

"Bonus gift?"

Now I smirk sinfully to myself. "My cock was your first gift."

She coughs a laugh as she stays focused on her work. "I was waiting for you to say something to take us there."

"We've been occupied today. Couldn't exactly say anything inappropriate."

"True. You know Enzo told my brother that we were all together today."

It piques my interest. "Oh yeah? What did Seb say?"

"Not much. He was unreadable, actually. But I think he believes that I hate you so much that it was literally Enzo and me helping you in a time of dire need."

I take a deep breath. "Do you still hate me?"

She peeks her head around a few scant branches and chortles a laugh. "The answer is kind of obvious, no? Was I not naked in your bed this morning?"

"Just checking. I would hate to get coal in my stockings, which I'm thankful as fuck that my mom texted to tell me that she is bringing stockings."

Her deep concentration on the tree is impressive. "I'm going to wrap some presents later for Enzo. You have the box of stuff."

"You would look kind of hot in wrapping paper only." That fantasy is building in my mind. Add in some heels and I'm a goner.

"I'll see if I have any left."

Not exactly a no.

"Tyler." She says my name as if it's a warning.

"What?"

She pulls gently on the lights. "You totally knotted the string of lights together."

My eyes drop down to where the level of lights end, and in truth, I wasn't paying that much attention, but now that I see it, I realize Santa just added another lump of coal to my stocking. Because it's a mess. Crossed strings, knots, weird patterns.

"Ooh. Sorry about that."

Her mouth turns into an O shape. "Are you serious? I'm trying to help, and you decide to ruin the lights." She's annoyed now but still seems in good spirits... I think.

I laugh, but maybe I shouldn't. "What? I'm sorry. You know this is all new territory for me."

Lainey drops the lights in her hands. "Will you stop this holiday grumbly monster grr roar routine?"

I'm trying to say the sentence in my head to see if it makes sense, but all I get is that she is irritated.

"Are you trying to just start an argument for old times' sake? Because you'll meet your match," I warn her, but I am completely bemused.

"Tyler, you grew up with parents who love the holidays, so suck it up, put in the effort, and get this damn tree decorated."

"No need to be feisty." It's hot.

She gripes as she gives up on the lights and opts to pick up a box of ornaments. "Let's just get this done. Otherwise, I'm going to demand that you do this while wearing only a towel."

Reminds me of the kiss when she dropped off cookies. Towels tend to do things to women.

"I can arrange that."

"Work," she snaps back.

For the next little while, she supervises my tree skills until we both hang ornaments in random spots. Stepping back, we both seemed satisfied with our work. To be honest, the tree looks a little wonky, but the effort is there.

"Just need the star for the top," she mentions and searches in the bag and pulls it out.

"Come here."

I haul her to me with her back to my front and my hands squaring her hips. Lifting her up high, she reaches for the top to connect the star to the pointed branch. Slowly I bring her back down, her body sliding against mine. With her feet back on the ground, I keep her still and wrap her close, kissing that place just below her earlobe.

"Thank you," I whisper.

She twists in my arms. "We have five minutes."

Our minds are synced, because next thing, we're going at it like two bears.

Kissing hard, hands racing to remove clothing, stumbling together. We have to catch our balance when we nearly run into the tree.

"Shit," Lainey hisses.

We save ourselves, and I'm too eager for her that I begin to lead us down to the floor as we kiss, and our knees lower at the same time with our mouths sealed together.

Her nails are scratching down my back, and I lead her legs to wrap around my waist. We are in such a fury of uncontrollable need that the moment I sheathe on the condom, she's already pushing her hips up, making it easy for me to slide right into her.

We're not going slow on this one, instead pure feral need. A reward for keeping our hands off of one another all day until now.

As I pump in and out of her, I notice something new.

Her eyes darting straight into mine are more beautiful with a glint of decorative light and a shade of a new mood when it comes to me.

But even better is that I notice this because she's underneath me and I'm inside of her… with a strong feeling in my chest to trust what is transpiring between us.

CHAPTER 13
LAINEY

I drop the rolls of wrapping paper carelessly on the floor. Tyler stands with arms crossed in the middle of his living room, and he's staring at me strangely.

"Okay, there?"

Kicking a tube, I have to admit the obvious. "Believe it or not, but I hate wrapping."

He takes satisfaction from this. "Ah, Miss Holiday Cheer has something she despises about the holiday."

I'm not impressed with his taunt, albeit kind of funny. "I'll wrap the gifts as fast as I can. Enzo is playing at the neighbor's downstairs, and I have about an hour window."

"I would say if Santa needs a helper then I'm your guy, but the only thing I can do is relax you by means that will not be beneficial to your wrapping session."

"But if I finish early then maybe you will be rewarded," I challenge him and flash my eyes.

He scoffs a sound with his grin, and his arms fall to hanging as he begins to leave. "As much as I would love to be rewarded, I need to run to the grocery store before my parents get here. My mom is crazy about having those biscuits that come in a tube and you bake in the oven. It's her Christmas Day breakfast ritual."

For a moment, I can't help but admire Tyler. His grumpy holiday modus is a façade—well, maybe, because he really hates trees and has already complained about the pine needles on the floor and overly sparkly ornaments. That's beside the point. This guy does these things to make his family happy. Actually, he does a lot of things to make people happy, and he just brushes it off.

He didn't have to hide gifts for me or let Enzo pick the ugliest tree, but Tyler acts as if it's no big deal.

Tyler snaps his fingers and quickly disappears into the kitchen, only to return a few moments later with a bag that he hands to me. "Here. Take it all."

I look curiously inside and choke on a laugh because it's meat, and some leftover Halloween candy in the shape of a pig. "Is this a bag of pork?"

"I need to empty my house." Creases form on my forehead, and he notices. "It has nothing to do with pork. Well, I mean, I thought an animal the shape of a pig might be insensitive to the holiday, but I need to get rid of all meat, plus anything that might remind us of animals in the kitchen. My aunt lives off of some spiritual rabbit food."

"You mean she is vegetarian?" I humorously correct him.

He lifts a shoulder. "Oh yeah, that's a thing. I mean, I guess we can call her that too."

I chuckle, and I'm amused by his borderline adorableness. Setting the bag to the side, I move us past it. "Don't forget about everything on the list I made you." I decided to help him out and just wrote down everything he would need at the store without explanation.

He pulls out the folded paper from the back pocket of his

jeans. "Got it. All twenty items with the reminder that eggnog is optional."

Giggling to myself, my eyes follow his movements of sliding his coat off the back of the stool. I hate to be the one to point it out, but I love his grumbles. "It's one of the busiest days of the year to step into a grocery store. I wish you strength."

His tongue sweeps across his upper teeth, his face tense. Tyler is well aware of that fact. He throws on his coat and checks he has his phone and keys. "Not sure you'll be here when I get back, but just let me know when I need to drop the presents off later."

Sitting on the ground, I search for the scissors that I brought with me. "Ah, it's okay. Just need to keep Enzo out of my closet for another twelve hours until he goes to sleep," I assure him and briefly look up to give him a tiny smile which he returns before he goes.

With a deep breath, setting holiday music on the Bluetooth and conquering my fights with the tape, I managed to wrap gifts, and I'm adding bows on my last two presents. I can't help but smile to myself as I hum along with the holiday song.

The bell in the song fades because an actual doorbell takes over.

Hopping up on my feet, I walk to the door and look through the peephole and see a couple that must be in their fifties. I have a strange feeling that these people are meant to be here.

Turning the knob, I paste on a giant smile when I open the door. "Hello."

The woman with darker hair and Tyler's eyes seems puzzled, but her pleasant smile stays put. Gosh, I hope I look like her when I'm that age. Her dewy skin is glowing, and her perfume is floral but subtle, maybe even with a hint of honey. The man has peppered gray hair but still seems to be in shape. Geez, I'm not sure I'm supposed to be thinking about the silver fox vibes.

"Oh, hi there," she greets me.

"Uh, you would be?" The man seems confused in an amusing way.

The woman reaches her perfectly manicured nails out to touch my arm. "You're the girlfriend. I knew he was keeping something from us. He's been too upbeat for his standards lately."

Quickly, I step to the side. "Oh." I laugh. "I'm Lainey, the neighbor from across the hall."

She assesses me from head to toe. "Huh."

The man offers me his hand, and I shake it. "Nice to meet you. We're Tyler's parents, Josh and Layla."

Layla is already hanging up her coat. "It is lovely to meet you. We're early, and I'm sure our son will release a long sentence of profanities at us. Where is he?"

I walk further down the hall, following them. "He went to the grocery store."

"Eek." She winces. "His nightmare."

His parents must have been here before because they need no direction of where to go and wander straight to the living room.

"I'll get the bags from the car later." Josh sits down on a couch near the large window.

Layla notices the floor which looks like a warzone as she joins her husband.

I feel the need to quickly explain. "Sorry it's a mess. Tyler was letting me hide my son's gifts from Santa here, and I needed to wrap them."

"Ah, Enzo, right?" his mother asks.

"Yeah, Enzo." I smile proudly, but my eyes must hint that I'm perplexed.

She notices. "He's mentioned him a few times since you moved in."

"Really?" Why does it hit me with a pleasant feeling in my chest.

"Mm-hmm." She makes it seem as though it's no big deal.

I drop down onto the other sofa as I think about her tidbit of information. "Well, he is a special kid."

"I'm sure," Josh affirms, and they both seem to be watching me as though they know something that I do not.

Fidgeting with my sweater, I'm not sure what to do. "Want something to drink?" I offer, even though this isn't my home.

His mother attempts to keep her smirk from growing. "It seems you know the layout of his home quite well."

This woman has a theory in her head, and I feel my cheeks warm.

Luckily, I'm saved by the sound of the front door opening, and I finally let go of the breath that I was apparently holding.

"Lainey, are you still here?" I hear Tyler call out, as he must be setting the bags of groceries down and taking off his coat. "I decided the roll of holiday cookies for the oven were also needed. Snowman-shaped, so I can cover my holiday bases. Do I get my reward?"

I smile tightly to myself because that last sentence is open to many interpretations. One look at his parents and my face drops from embarrassment because I realize what route of thought they followed.

"Ah fuck. The coats," he says, and then we hear his footsteps, and all of our heads swing, waiting for Tyler to grasp the current dynamic. "They're here early," he states as he rounds the corner.

"Clearly dampening your reward opportunities." His mom jumps up and opens her arms for a hug as she walks straight to him.

"Layla," Tyler's dad warns her under his breath.

She ignores him and gives Tyler a bear hug. The type that I give Enzo on a daily basis.

"Lainey, this is my mom. She doesn't have a filter," Tyler mentions blandly.

She swats her son. "Be nice or no presents for you."

Tyler walks to his dad who stands, and they side-hug.

His mom spots something near the wall and beelines straight to the table. "What's this?"

I stand to assess what she means. "Enzo made that. Apparently, your son needs a menorah for tomorrow, and Tyler didn't have many options."

She brings her hand to her heart and coos. "Adorable. It's perfect."

Shrugging a shoulder, I do my best to maintain my mom pride. "I mean, I'm not sure how secure those foil holders are, so you may want to consider not burning down the building, but it works."

"Trust me, you should be more concerned by my husband's sister, Harper."

Tyler's lightly winces. "Here it goes."

"Layla, you love her, so don't," Josh warns.

"What? I think she's great, but sometimes it gets a little, well… out there. Remember when we had to drink moon water for your birthday party that she threw?"

Now I'm lost. "What is moon water?"

"Water you leave out at night by the window to accept the

light of the moon to help you not age… apparently," Tyler flatly explains.

The dynamic of this family is hilarious, and as much as I would love to stay, I shouldn't be here. I'm just the neighbor… right?

"Well, I'll let you all catch up. I'll just quickly get the presents out of here."

"No need to rush on our account," his father clarifies.

Tyler shakes his head because I'm well aware that this is all kind of awkward, and his parents don't seem like people who will let it go.

"You and Enzo should join us tomorrow." His mother sounds enthusiastic and insistent.

I whip my sight to Tyler whose eyes are wide. Luckily, I can answer without an excuse. "That is kind of you, but we are going to a friend's in the morning."

She claps her hands together. "Then the afternoon."

"Mom," Tyler mutters under his breath.

Of course he wouldn't be happy. We're only two people who hook up and can enjoy moments as friends. It's not a meeting-family situation.

"What?" She looks at her son as though he is crazy. "Nothing wrong with having a *friend* over."

Ah fuck, she just threw logic at us.

Tyler holds my gaze. "Lainey and Enzo are, of course, welcome. In fact, save us all and join us."

"I, uh, oh." I swallow in defeat. "Okay."

The entire room goes quiet because his mother just strong-armed us all, and she's happy as a clam.

"I'm going to head out." I swoop down to grab a few presents and the bag of meat.

"I'll help you." Tyler joins me and picks up the biggest box.

We manage to ignore them both as we quickly scoot away out of the living room until we have to stop because the bags of groceries are a barricade by the front door, and we place the presents down.

"I'm so sorry," Tyler says quietly so only we can hear, and he sounds completely guilty, but he shouldn't feel that way. "I didn't know they were arriving early."

I chuckle and smile. "Your parents are… unique."

"Tell me about it." He blows out a breath.

"It's fine, we don't have to stop by tomorrow." I'm giving him an out.

He shakes his head. "Nah, it will be fun. You two should stop by."

"Really?" My voice pitches higher.

"I mean, they are a pack of vultures who are eager for every detail of my life, but I'm hoping the presence of a child and a game of dreidel will deter them and keep them occupied."

I clink my tongue. "Smart. Okay, what can we bring?"

"Sanity," he deadpans, and my smile returns. "Seriously, nothing."

For a moment we stay silent, except our eyes have their own conversation. One where we recognize that the situation between us is shifting. We're not the same two people around one another as we were a month ago. Neither one of us seems to mind.

"Even if I don't kiss you now, I'm sure my mom will plant mistletoe strategically around the place by tomorrow afternoon," he explains casually and leans against the door.

"My mouth might be busy." I bite my inner cheek.

He whistles out a sound. "Just had to take us there, huh?"

With purpose, I push out my chest and put on my best sultry face and voice. "Yes." I step to him and kiss his cheek before brushing my mouth to his ear. "Enjoy your evening."

My intention was to only kiss his cheek and rile him a little with a whisper, but he moves the angle of his head to capture my lips for a quick kiss.

Except the kiss will still leave an effect on me. I'll still be smiling like a girl with a crush for the rest of the night. Most of all, my mind will be racing with possibilities of what we are.

Being only friends with benefits is the lie of the century. It isn't possible.

When he pulls away, it's as if his eyes are giving me an unknown promise. His mouth twitches because he is aware that he has a pull on me.

It's a few seconds before we break our moment and handle the logistics of the bags.

Five minutes later, with presents hidden in my closet, I double-check the stockings above the fireplace. They are perfectly in place as they have been for weeks, but I need to occupy myself. It's hopeless because my mind is lost on one person. Enzo is safe and happy, which is why it feels okay that I'm allowed to have moments where I can only think of one other person. The hockey guy living across the hall.

ENZO IS SO ENGROSSED in his new remote-controlled race car that I ignore the scattered opened boxes and paper everywhere but admire the twinkling of tree lights on this Christmas morning.

I'm resting on the sofa in pajamas, with my feet tucked under my knees. Cup of coffee in one hand and my phone in the other while I sit at the kitchen island.

"Sorry. Santa's gifts veto calls with uncles," I tell my brother as we talk over video, and Enzo says merely a hello before returning to his presents.

He chuckles and scratches his scruff. I wish he would trim his beard. It isn't long and maybe borderline stubble, but I don't think it suits him.

"I'll accept that. Happy he got the race car." My brother grins.

"Way to go, overshadowing Santa," I tease him. I do my best to have a little order to holiday presents for Enzo. Something he wants, something he needs but has no clue he needs it, something practical, something to wear, and one extra toy that I think he might enjoy. Seb? His rule is to go for the most overpriced electronic toy there is. The wheels will ruin the floor, but it's Seb's place, so his responsibility.

"I'm going to have to head off. I need to get dressed before we head to a colleague's for brunch."

My son perks his head up. "I'm hungry. Hey, Uncle Seb, we're going to Tyler's later!" he calls out before returning to his toy.

My lips roll in then quirk out, before I face the screen to notice Seb's face has gone blank.

"It's nothing. He has his parents in from out of town, and they invited us for Hanukkah stuff later." I do my best to downplay this.

Lines form on his forehead. "Tyler's Jewish?" But he quickly shakes away curiosity and turns serious. "Why have you been spending more time with him?"

"It's a grandmother of a grandmother kind of thing," I explain the first part of the question and avoid his real question.

"Okay. And the second part of that question? Bjorn already told me that you arrived at his holiday party with

Tyler. I was just waiting for you to tell me yourself. So let me repeat: Why are you spending time with Tyler?"

I take a quick sip of my coffee to give myself time. "We've just been hanging out. Holidays and helping with Enzo. He needed a tree and, of course, trees with lights are not his thing."

My brother's eyes squeeze and his nostrils flare. I can tell that he is having his own internal conversation. "Fine. But if there is something more, then he better do the honorable thing and talk to me."

I shush him instantly and nearly jump off the couch and race to the kitchen. "Will you be quiet. Enzo was in earshot," I scold him in a hushed tone.

"Fair enough."

It's not a good idea for Enzo to get ideas that there is more going on with Tyler. To Enzo, we're neighbors, that's it.

"Listen, there is nothing to talk about, and I really need to go."

He shakes his head. "Avoidance, Lainey. You're my sister. I know you."

"Is that so? Oh no, my coffee is cold. Need to get Enzo dressed. Oops, need to take the casserole for brunch out of the oven. Have a great day with your girlfriend, bye now." I string the sentence together then hang up and set the phone down on the counter as if it's a hot potato.

The last thing I need right now is to discuss Tyler with Seb.

Blowing out an exhausting breath, I do notice that the time says we need to go in thirty minutes.

Half an hour later and repeated asks that Enzo brush his teeth, and we're opening the door. I'm balancing the egg casserole that I promised to bring, and Enzo is busy pulling on his hat.

"A present." My son is diving down to the doormat before I can even check what he is talking about.

Lo and behold, there is a present wrapped in Hanukkah paper. I know instantly who it is for, and Tyler must have run out of the other wrapping paper that he got.

"It's for me. My name is on it." Enzo is ripping through the paper before I can even protest. "Whoa… it's the hockey rink edition of my model blocks."

Be still my little heart. My entire insides melt. It is so incredibly thoughtful. My gaze travels to his front door then back to my son who has a goofy grin on his face.

I'm feeling more attached, and I'm beginning to realize that I'm comfortable with this feeling. It's not scary, only exhilarating.

That's the best Chrismukkah Day gift possible.

CHAPTER 14
TYLER

How I've survived three hours so far, I'm not entirely sure. Aunt Harper and my mom have been waiting for their moment to corner and interrogate me. The clock is no longer in my favor.

My dad and uncle are in the living room discussing stocks, which is as boring to me as sitting in the kitchen and peeling the potatoes for the latkes. Love the latkes but can't stand peeling potatoes. Surely, there is a machine for this? Or they are simply hiding it to trap me longer.

The day started simple and easy. I had coffee and biscuits with my parents, and we opened a few gifts by the Christmas tree. Nothing crazy. We don't do elaborate and instead opt for small things. Cliché sweaters, that kind of thing.

Staring down at the potato, I'm at my final peel. The moment that I drop the peeler, my aunt flicks her dark hair over her shoulder and glances at me as she continues to flip the latkes in the pan.

"So."

Here it comes. My mom sitting on the other side of the island covers her smirk by keeping her mouth as shut as possible. I know how this goes, have my Aunt Harper do my mom's dirty work. Then again, Harper is always ready for any gossip.

"You mentioned a neighbor… a woman… a good-looking one that is stopping by." Oh, subtle.

"Did I say good-looking?" I reply blandly, purely because I'm aware that I shouldn't slip in any details that they will use as ammunition.

"No, but your mom did. Tell me more. I need all the deets before she arrives later." My family never ages, and I cringe when they attempt to use language that should just be criminal coming out of their mouths.

"Lainey is a neighbor with a cute kid. She's a preschool teacher, and her brother used to play for my team but was traded. There. You have the *deets*."

She turns off the stove, as she's about to get comfortable and fire safety comes first.

"Single?"

"Yes," my mom jumps in, and my eyes slide to her. She shrugs at me. "What? I have my ways of detecting these things, plus you talk about her all the time."

"I do not." My voice sounds a little uneven because I just lied.

My aunt snaps her fingers. "He's doing that thing, Layla. The look away, squeak in his voice, and his words sound completely unbelievable. He always used to do it when he and his cousin would get wild at family gatherings."

"Us, wild?" I scoff then look around my place. Eggnog with an extra dash of rum was opened promptly upon their arrival before my aunt took the liberty to spread Hanukkah-themed confetti on my table to make it bluer.

"Someone must have broken through your outer layer. You have a Christmas tree, for Christ's sake."

"Harper, don't say the Lord's name in vain." My mom has never stepped foot in a church.

My aunt snaps her gaze to my mother. "It's fine. Jesus is our favorite Jewish carpenter, remember?"

I rub my temples. Keeping up with these women and their fast conversations is a headache.

"Let's not bother Tyler. He doesn't have many days off during the season, so let him enjoy it," my mother attempts to deter my aunt.

"Yeah, a chance to *relax*," I deadpan.

My aunt throws her hands in the air. "Fine. But I'm on to you." She points her spatula at me. "I love that she's a teacher. We'll have so much to talk about." Shit. My aunt is a kindergarten teacher; she and Lainey will hit it off.

"Riveting."

It's not that I don't want Lainey and Enzo to stop by, I do. My family being present isn't ideal. First off, they are an energy drain, and secondly, they will be observing us to prove their theories right. I can't forget that Lainey and I are kind of in a confusing state. Neighbors, friends, hooking up. That's what we're doing, right?

In the end, it's not about me. Enzo was curious when we were tree shopping about Chrismukkah, so it will be nice for him. They also live across the hall and have an easy escape if needed.

But maybe it is about me. An intuitive selfish want to have Lainey around. I only have a few days off, and I want to enjoy them, and that seems to entail having Lainey nearby. Yesterday was relaxed and simple. Making lists, checking them twice, and watching her cute expression when it involved wrapping. We didn't need to go to any expensive restaurants or make a big deal of the day. I hear what some of the guys on my team do for their significant others, and to me, it's over the top. If I were to get Lainey a designer bag, I'm positive she would throw it back at me.

The next hour is busy in my head. We eat the latkes, a nut roast since turkey is not on the menu, and my mom made homemade cranberry sauce. I make no mistake of the hours on the clock, and when my aunt and mom are busy in the kitchen cleaning up, I rush to the doorbell when I assume that it is Lainey arriving.

Opening the door, I press a smile with my lips. "Welcome."

"Hey, Tyler, thanks for the gift. It's awesome." Enzo seems excited and races into my home before I get a chance to respond. It's kind of funny.

"Sorry. He's been talking about this the entire ride home," Lainey explains.

I place my hand on her shoulder and grab her attention. "Just give me a sign when it's too much or feel free to fake an illness when they have zero filter," I say in a hushed tone.

She chuckles under her breath. "I'm sure it's fine. Right?" She begins to doubt.

"Tyler," my aunt sing-songs my name.

I grumble to myself and indicate with my head for Lainey to follow me. When we reach the living room, it seems that Enzo has already introduced himself because this kid has confidence and is always fearless, which he could have only gotten from his mom.

"What a little gentleman you have," my mom compliments Lainey.

"Good to see you both again. Merry Christmas," Lainey gives a little wave to my dad, "and Happy Hanukkah," she greets my aunt and uncle.

"I'm Harper, and this is Max," my aunt introduces herself.

"We ate ham for brunch, but my mom said I wasn't

supposed to say that," Enzo almost proudly says before running to the table where he must spot the sufganiyot donuts that my mom brought from a special bakery in Chicago.

Lines of awkwardness form on Lainey's face. "Sorry about that."

My dad waves her off. "It's fine. I snuck a piece of bacon this morning that Tyler forgot to pack in your bag. Besides, it's also Christmas and not your dietary requirements."

"I'm vegetarian. One with the animals, you know. Tyler tells me that you are a teacher. So am I." My aunt is already scooting down the couch and patting the spot next to her, indicating that Lainey has no choice but to join her for a chat.

Lainey happily joins her.

Maybe this will all be alright. Everyone returns to their conversations, and I walk to Enzo who is indeed eyeing the donuts. "See something you like?"

"Yes. Are these the ones with jam in the middle?" he asks as if he is an expert.

"Yep. My weakness, I could eat about five," I admit. When the dough is fluffy enough and the jam proportion is generous and the powdered sugar soft, I'm a goner. Thank goodness for cheat days.

My mother touches my shoulder as she joins me and looks down at Enzo. "Grab a plate for him." She gives Enzo a big smile.

"Don't worry. That was already in the plan."

She rubs my back. "You know, your mood changed the moment they arrived."

"Enlighten me how."

"I've never seen you this way. That's a good thing."

And she's right.

❄

Lainey endured my aunt babbling her ear off for a solid half-hour. Enzo stuffed his face with latkes and donuts, and I'm positive he will have a stomach ache later. He seemed fascinated when my aunt lit the fourth candle. With the excitement of Lainey's arrival and the traditions out of the way, we are all enjoying a drink in my living room.

I love Matchbox IPAs, and I was lucky that my uncle Max brought me a case of their new blend. Sitting on the arm of the sofa, Lainey is next to me and sipping on her wine.

"In all honesty, your son was my worst nightmare as a neighbor," Lainey explains when my dad asks a question about first impressions.

My dad takes a sip of his scotch. "I couldn't stand Layla when I first met her, either. Plus, her brother was going to kill me anyhow."

"I'm sure Seb won't kill Tyler." She eases his worries with a smile.

My mother lifts her nose as though she just connected a dot. "Why would Seb want to kill my son?" She's onto us.

Lainey's mouth opens and a scratched sound leaves her throat. "Oh, I mean, on the ice, of course. They don't play on the same team anymore."

"Yeah, those hockey guys are a completely different species when they are on the ice," my dad comments, oblivious.

"To be honest, I was kind of surprised by the sparkle on the front door. I didn't take my nephew for a guy who enjoys garland," my uncle adds his thoughts.

Lainey stifles a laugh. "That's because I did it to annoy him."

"He also came to Thanksgiving and annoyed my mom, too." Everyone whips their attention to Enzo on the floor who is busy drawing.

"I thought you spent the day with a teammate," my mother grills me.

"That was the plan, but…"

Lainey pretends to glance at an invisible watch. "Look at the time. I probably need to head across the hall and get the little guy ready for bed. There is still wrapping paper scattered around the living room that needs to be cleaned up too."

I can't blame Lainey for faking a reason to escape. The room is closing in on us. She helps Enzo pack up his pencils and books before she makes her round saying goodbye to everyone.

As soon as I open my door, Enzo races across the hall and opens their unlocked door. She takes a step but then pauses and spins on her feet to face me. "That was fun."

My eyes widen, and I blow out a breath. "I mean, it was, just a lot, you know. They can be…"

"They're special." She means that sincerely.

I drag my thumb along my chin. "Yeah, they are. Detectives, but family. They always want what is best."

"Good."

My face sours, and I scratch the back of my head. "They might have this crazy idea that I'm really into you and we are a thing."

Her head retreats back slightly. "Is that a crazy idea?" She's testing me, I can see it. Maybe she is curious.

I'm just going to own this moment; a few seconds pass, and my face eases into a soft smile. "Yeah…" My voice is delicate, even I recognize it. "I am into you."

She absorbs my words then steps closer, peeking over my shoulder to ensure nobody has snuck into the hallway behind me to watch us. Lainey brings her warm palm up to cup my cheek. "I think I like that." The corner of her mouth tugs because we are both in agreement.

Her finger points up. "You weren't joking about the strategic mistletoe."

I follow her line of sight, and my mouth drops open. Someone must have just put that there because that was not there two hours ago.

"I'm supposed to be enjoying the holiday cheer, so in that case." I lean in to give her a respectable but long kiss on her cheek. Chaste with a hint of wicked.

We enter our little world again where time stops and our eyes tie together.

"I guess you are away for games the next few days."

I nod. "I am. We even have a game on New Year's Eve. It's a 2pm game, but we probably won't get back to Illinois until late. Not the first time I've missed when the clock strikes midnight."

She doesn't say anything. Maybe she was hoping that we could spend it together, or at least I was hoping we could spend it together.

"Doesn't sound cool. We're going to a New Year's party a few floors down. The parents of Enzo's friend are throwing one. It'll be easy to get Enzo in bed after midnight," she explains.

She'll do anything for him, but maybe I sense that in a different time and place, it wouldn't be the way that she would celebrate. I wish I could change that. The celebration part.

"Well, I should get back inside," I mention, but I would rather be here.

"Me too."

Neither one of our feet moves. I can't help it, I lean in to kiss her mouth, but she meets me halfway because she wants it too. This isn't a soft kiss, it's wild, reckless, and I trap her against the wall next to my door. I kiss under her jaw then back up to crash my lips onto her mouth. Her hands land on my hips, and she jerks me closer.

But I'm aware where we are and do my best to unglue our mouths. Her mouth is red and swollen which means my mouth must be a mess. Our breathing is heavy and everything about it screams that I would take her to bed right now if I could.

Alas, all I can do is enjoy her angelic smile. "Happy Chrismukkah, Tyler."

"Happy Chrismukkah." I grin.

She heads inside her apartment, and I wait for her door to click closed before taking a breath to stabilize myself and return to my place.

I'm closing my door behind me when I nearly jump because I'm startled.

"Tyler, a word." My mom sounds stern, and she never has in my entire life. She's standing at the end of the hallway waiting for me.

Walking to her, she stands with her arms crossed where the hallway meets the living room.

"Yes, dearest mother."

She pokes my chest with her finger. "She's the one."

"Excuse me."

"Lainey, she's the one. Despite your aunt's theory that her cards and the position of the moon was telling her that Lainey is your one." My mom seems to shudder at that idea. "My theory isn't one at all. It's fact. The way you look at her, the way she looks at you, that kid is adorable, and most of all, you are so happy, and it gives me joy. Even if you haven't figured it out yet, you will. Others sometimes see it first."

I bite my cheek, and I'm unable to give a reply.

"You have your hockey career to be a grumpy chunk of steel. Off the ice, you no longer have to be that way. You found your key, and it isn't just the holidays putting you in this mode—because let's be honest, come garbage day for tree pickup on January fifth, then you will be rejoicing—but it's Lainey. Someone would have to be blind not to see it. As your mother, I'm telling you not to let her go."

"You got all of that from just a few hours?" She nods confidently. I inhale a deep breath. "I hear you." That's the generic answer that I give.

She wiggles her finger at me. "Good. New Year's and Valentine's Day are now part of your calendar because you have someone to celebrate it with."

Her hands form a ball, and she brings them to her heart. "This is the best gift to see you this way," she gushes.

And she's right.

I'm beginning to understand how I have gotten the best gift.

CHAPTER 15
TYLER

First practice after a few days off wasn't as brutal as I thought. All of the guys seem to be in a good headspace, and we are ready to conquer the rest of the season.

Returning home after morning practice, I walk down the hall to my front door and instantly smile when I see Lainey and Enzo. Lainey has the door open as Enzo ties his shoe. I was expecting to see them, as Lainey mentioned maybe we could meet up for a bit.

Enzo peers up and a wide grin greets me. "Tyler! Did Mom tell you that we are going to do another night of Hanukkah? We'll light a candle later when we have dinner."

"Sure. Where are you off to?" I say as I stop in front of my door.

Lainey flashes her eyes at me. "Enzo was invited to play at a friend's. He won't be with us until dinner time."

I'm on her wavelength. I'm happy to spend time with him, and since he will be with us for dinner, then I don't feel guilty that I get his mom all to myself.

"Oh, okay." I nod.

I hear the sound of a door opening, and I glance over my shoulder to see another little boy at the end of the hall where the stairs are. Enzo quickly runs off.

"Behave and use please and thank you," Lainey calls out as Enzo disappears.

She shakes her head, amused. "His friend lives downstairs," she explains.

I saunter toward Lainey, and I cradle her face in my hands while I steal a soft kiss.

Pulling away from one another proves difficult as our mouths are magnets, unwilling to part.

She begins to step, forcing me to walk back. "Open your door, please," she says against my lips.

I turn and do as I'm told, while she closes her own door.

She follows me inside, and we seem relaxed as we head into the living room. Lainey pauses and assesses the tree.

"You've marked the garbage day when trees can be thrown to the curb, right?" She cringes.

"Have you lied to me all of this time and think the tree is ugly?"

"No, of course not." There is a lie in there. Her lips smack together a few times. "Just doing my neighborly duty to check that you are informed of city calendars."

Walking to her, I appreciate her tact. "Thank you for your concern." I can't help it, I need to touch her. Wrapping my arms around her feels comforting. "What's on the docket for this afternoon? Want to watch a movie? Drag me to the grocery store to get things for dinner? Let me watch you cook in hopefully nothing but an apron?" I nonchalantly list options.

Her bottom lip gets trapped. "Actually…" She trails off.

"Yes?" I coax.

A mischievous look which I've never seen grace her face

before appears on her beautiful cheeks and mouth. "Since we are celebrating another night of Hanukkah, then I guess you get a gift, and I kind of had something in mind." The moment she begins to slither down my body, my arms go slack, and I'm fully on board with this gift.

Lainey is on her knees with her doe eyes peering up at me and her fingers touching my belt.

I swallow my excitement to keep me in place, but my dick already raised to the occasion about three seconds ago. "I've told you how much I enjoy your mind, right?"

Her lips part, and she hums in agreement as she begins to unbuckle my belt. Fuck this. I quickly help her get my belt off with more speed. The sound of the belt clasp being undone is all we hear. Her delicate fingers sneak between my boxer briefs and my hips to peel my jeans lower. My cock springs free, and the glee in this woman's eyes should be criminal.

Lainey's tongue darts out and swirls around my tip, and I groan from the sensitive touch that is barreling need throughout my body. She wraps her hand around the base of my cock and takes me further into her wet mouth.

She sucks, and her lips pop off. "Who needs candy canes to suck on when I have you," she rasps before she licks me like a piece of candy.

Raking my fingers through her hair, I'm desperate for her. "You look really good with your mouth stuffed with my cock." I guide her as her mouth takes me fully. Her lips wrap tighter around my shaft because she's a good girl.

She learns my rhythm, and even when she begins to gag and I try to back away, she just sinks her nails into my ass to keep me in place. This isn't a show, she wants this. To please me, and I can't wait to go down on her after this.

Her mouth is wet and warm and tight around my cock.

The way she stares at me while she continues to suck feels as though she is seeking approval. "Beautiful. Such a good girl."

We continue in this moment, and I'm beginning to wonder if I just left earth. My body tightens and fire builds below my navel. Every sense of my cock is heightened in sensitivity. A barrel of a release.

"I'm going to come." I let her hair go, giving her space to give me one more lick, but Lainey doesn't back down. She sucks and keeps her mouth fixed on me. A slew of curses leave me as I release into her mouth. I feel as though I might black out.

My breath is rapid, my heart racing, and Lainey is beautiful on her knees before me. She pulls away only to smile as she swallows.

How the hell am I still standing?

"What the fuck just happened?" I attempt to catch my breath as she stands.

"Holiday magic." Her smirk is sly.

Pulling up my pants, I take a moment. She was determined and so am I. "You better get on that kitchen counter right now," I direct.

She wiggles her finger side to side. "Nuh-uh. I actually do have to go to the grocery store and wanted you to come with."

I step to her, plant my hands on her shoulders, and brush a kiss against her forehead. "Afterwards then. You have no idea how sexy you are."

She sputters a laugh. "I don't know." She grows shy. "Maybe I didn't realize I have it in me, but I wanted to do it."

"I am not sure any of that makes sense."

She playfully slaps my arm. "I just mean that you have all of these girls probably fawning over you. Then there is me who just…" Her shoulder rolls back. "My experience is… well, you know…"

I'm quick to capture her chin with my hooked finger to tip her face up and ensure we have direct eye contact. "Everything in that sentence makes zero sense. I'm not like those guys who have a party all the time. You saying you have no experience is a lie. You just made me come in what can only be described as an out-of-body experience."

She bobbles her head side to side. "Fine… you're believable."

I kiss her forehead again. "It's the truth. Now can I show you?" I softly plead.

Her smile is bright. "Tempting, however time is not on our side. Enzo is only away for so long, and I really need to go to the store. And maybe…" She squeezes my arms. "I want to see your new grocery store skills in action."

I laugh. "Hey, I made it out alive on Christmas Eve. I think I can handle a weekday shop."

"Good. Now come on."

Twenty minutes later, we are cruising the aisles of the grocery store making a turn into the pasta aisle. Everything felt strange as we were throwing juice boxes, kids' snacks, and yogurt cups into the cart. Then I realized it was strange because it felt right. The items were a reminder of the joy I experience when I'm around Lainey and Enzo.

I'm not paying attention, until Lainey says my name and holds up a box of pasta.

"Spaghetti is fine, right? For your macros and Hulk diet."

It's sweet that she thinks of the little things. "Kind of you to ask but don't plan a meal around the demands of my pain-in-the-ass trainer. Spaghetti is perfect, though. Carbs, classic, and I assume Enzo won't complain."

She tosses the box into the cart. "Perfect. It will pair

nicely with those chocolate coins you threw into the cart when I wasn't looking."

I grin and shrug. "I mean, we need to have the necessities if we are doing another night of Hanukkah."

"Fair enough."

We continue to push the cart and move along. The next aisle is laundry detergent, and I grab a bottle. I side-eye Lainey when I hear her choke on a laugh.

"What's wrong?"

She smiles wistfully in honesty. "It's just… kind of weird yet normal that I'm seeing you in everyday life."

"Explain."

Her shoulder lifts. "I guess… this is just everyday life, and we seem okay to conquer a grocery store together. It's a sort of ease, do you know what I mean?"

I press my lips then nod with a smile. "I do. It's crossed my mind a few times in the yogurt aisle, cereal aisle, and my disappointment that you picked pretzels instead of those fish-shaped crackers that I could steal from Enzo when he has a snack. They are even red- and green-colored for the season."

"Uh-oh, I just learned your cracker preference. That runs deep."

I roll my eyes and continue our journey.

Because she's right on the deep front. It's so simple yet meaningful.

We've come undone around one another. Breaking down walls and falling into a place that I didn't know existed but feels so right.

I'm not sure what to call it.

But until I figure it out, I'll only be snacking on pretzels.

CHAPTER 16
LAINEY

My mouth closes then opens, only to snap closed again. I'm staring at Gracie as we sit on my couch. It's New Year's Eve and Enzo is sick with a bug. All plans for the night have resulted in me wearing pajamas with Chinese food on the way. It's okay, I kind of enjoy the cozy feeling of doing nothing.

Gracie waits for me to say something to her earth-shattering news.

"P-pregnant?" I repeat what I think I heard her say.

"That I am." She quirks her lips out. To my surprise, she seems at ease with her unexpected news.

"And with the coach?" Again, did I really hear this right? She nods once.

"As in you and he are going to be parents."

Gracie gives me a blank stare. "You heard me the first time."

I touch her knee out of instinct to comfort. "How?"

"One of those annoying October storms of rain and sleet, finding shelter, and chewing on candy, you know how it goes. Then boom, a few weeks later you learn a baby is on the way.

A complete Chrismukkah miracle, right?" She smiles nervously then swallows and covers her mouth.

I quirk my lips out and tip my head to the side. She isn't wrong.

"You know what. Let's leave the baby talk for another time. I need a distraction, so can we talk about something else?"

"Sure. Just know that I'm here for you, and if you're happy, then so am I," I assure her.

"Thanks, but you are also happy because of a certain hockey player."

I try not to blush but fail, because nothing about her sentence is an unfair accusation.

"You were watching the locker room interviews after his game when I arrived."

I roll a shoulder back. "It was a tough game." They played hard and went into overtime, but unfortunately, the other team scored first.

"I told you my news, now catch me up. It's only fair."

I hesitate for a second, but then I'm giddy. "We're just neighbors who are friends who slept together and who spent the holidays with his family. No biggie." I reach for my mug of tea on the coffee table to avoid reading her expression but then decide to be honest. "I'm not sure what is going on between us, but it feels promising."

She grins and squeals because she is excited for me. "Will you spend New Year's together?"

Sipping my tea, I shake my head at the same time. "No. They have to travel back, and besides, I feel as though being together when the clock strikes midnight is kind of a big deal."

"It's romantic."

I press my lips together and roll them in as I recall what

has been running through my mind lately. "I kind of always thought that when I would be ready to really date again that I would freak out because I'm a single mom and need to find balance, but with Tyler, we just flow."

"That's a great sign."

"I sent him a text after the game. Just to say I was watching while Enzo is asleep and sick. Then sorry for the overtime loss, but at least they still got a point for the standings, then added a slew of emojis." And sending it came without thought. No second-guessing myself or wondering if I'm overstepping the lines between us. "I won't hear back from him, I'm sure. He's busy." Hockey is his life.

Gracie nudges my arm with her hand. "You two are good for one another and mellow each other out."

I snicker and smile. "That wasn't the case two months ago."

"Even better. You've seen one another during the not-so-stellar personality moments, yet here you both are."

Huh, I guess that is a good point.

"That theory is not bad," I admit.

She slowly begins to drag herself off my couch. "Now. On that note, time for me to head home."

"Thanks for stopping by. Are you sure you don't want to stay for dinner?"

Her palm flies up. "No way. The thought of food makes me want to hurl, and I want to drive before it gets too dark. Pajamas and sleep are the way I'm going to welcome the new year. I already know what the new year will bring, so I'm all good." She pats her stomach.

I love her positivity. She's the breath of fresh air that everyone needs in their life.

I stand to give her a hug and walk with her to my front

door. "Be safe, and we'll meet for coffee later in the week, okay?"

"Sounds good. Happy New Year! May it be the year for you with a hot boyfriend." She flashes her eyes at me.

"You too. May it be the year for you with an adorable healthy baby and a baby daddy that you are crazy about."

She smiles contritely at me. She knows that I'm teasing her about the baby daddy part, because she might not want to admit it but she's already in love.

The next few hours, I enjoy my winter cozy fest. Food is delivered later than expected, but I guessed as much since it's a busy night. Candles are lit, my favorite playlist is on, and I'm curled with a blanket and my e-reader. Maybe some would say this is boring, but it is so damn relaxing.

I've checked on Enzo a few times, but he is out like a light from the children's medicine. His fever is going down, at least. Probably just a passing virus that kids get. Luckily, I've become immune to many since I've been working in a preschool for a few years.

Sure, I notice the clock and the fact that midnight is approaching, and maybe a tiny piece of me wishes that I could celebrate it with a certain someone, but it's okay.

I find it strange how we all become fixated on a number on a clock. It's a mental block, I guess. A new year is a new chance.

The gentle knock on my door sparks my attention, and a spot in my heart fills with excitement because intuition just sparked it. I get up off the coach and keep the throw blanket wrapped around me. I'm in pajamas and big fluffy socks, but you can never be warm enough.

The moment I open the door, *whoosh.*

The world stops, and my entire body stills as I see Tyler

standing there. He's still in his post-game suit. His sexy grin is already weakening me in the knees.

"W-what are you doing here?"

"I'm here to celebrate New Year's."

My sight shoots down, and I realize my outfit, down to my fluffy snowman socks, is anything but hot. "I'm a mess."

"I love it. It's the socks that make the outfit." He winks at me then politely barges past me as if he owns the place.

I gingerly close the door and follow him to my living room. The way he unbuttons his suit blazer leaves my mouth watering, made worse when he rolls up his sleeves.

"Don't drool." He smirks at me, as he must understand where my mind just went.

"I thought you would be on the road."

"Luckily, we got in an hour early. So here I am."

My smile grows then falters. "You can't be here."

He looks at me strange, maybe almost hurt. "You don't want me here?"

Shaking my head, I join him as he sits down on the sofa. "It's not that. Enzo is sick, and I don't want you to catch it since you have games later in the week."

"It's fine." He doesn't seem worried. "How is he doing?"

I move to sit on one hip and face him. "Sleeping. I'm sure he will be fine in the morning. Are you hungry? I have left-over Chinese food. I kind of ate all the eggrolls, they're my favorite."

He touches the outer part of my thigh. "Who doesn't love eggrolls?"

We assess one another, trying to connect dots or say something first.

"I'm kind of happy you showed up," I admit.

His brows rise. "Kind of?"

"I *am* happy that you showed up."

"I was hoping we would be back early. I wanted to be here with you. Can I let you in on a secret?"

He leans in, and my heart races. The feeling of warmth from his body getting closer to me and the room getting smaller all feels too much, but my heart lifts. "I've been thinking about you non-stop."

I touch his shoulder because I want us to be connected in some way. "Me too."

An almost boyish grin appears. "Also been thinking about us too?"

"I have," I admit shyly.

He pecks a kiss on my forehead. "What's going on between us is too strong. I can't deny it. So what do we do about this? Because I have some ideas." His voice lowers, and it sends vibrations down my body.

I bite back my half-grin. "There is a chance that I'm in agreement with some of those ideas."

He pulls back a little, but we are still too close to be just friends. "We're more, Lainey. There doesn't need to be confusion about it. It's clear to me now, and I don't want us to go down the road of just benefits because I care for you too much, I want you too much. It's because of you that I have a fucking Christmas tree and handmade menorah even though holiday cheer isn't for me. But it's because of you that I changed that thought."

My cheeks tighten from my smile. "And I've forgotten what it was like when we would irritate one another. In fact, I've been calm and excited when I hear your name."

"Don't we deserve to explore this thing between us?"

"I have Enzo. It's not just—"

He cuts right in. "It's not just you, and I know that. You two are a package deal, and I wouldn't dream of anything else." There is no disappointment or doubt intertwined in his words.

My heart can't handle it because it's far too perfect, I'm far too lucky, but he is right in front of me and I have no reason to believe otherwise.

"Tyler, I needed to hear that maybe, and I want us to be together. Explore what is more for us." I squeeze his hand on my thigh. "We just have to be careful around Enzo. Give it some time before we spill the news, you know."

"Got it." He scoots closer to me.

I swoop in for a kiss, and he kisses me back with reverence. I could get lost in this the entire night, but there is a whisper in the back of my brain, and I pull away.

"Do you want the good news or bad news?" I ask, and Tyler looks at me peculiarly. "Good news is that we get to spend midnight together. Bad news, I only have juice boxes if you want to toast."

His head falls forward as he laughs before driving his sight up to my eyes. "Juice boxes are perfect. Feels kind of like a sign that this is the way that we should celebrate us for a new year."

I lick my lips with my smile not disappearing. I love his answer.

A minute later I'm back with two fruit punch juice boxes and flop onto the couch next to him. It's quite a scene to see Tyler still in his dress shirt and slacks, trying to jam the impossible straw into a juice box. Who knew that it could be a turn-on. Maybe because it embodies how insanely hot he is *and* great with kids.

"New Year's resolution?" I ask as we get comfortable.

"To avoid juice getting all over my post-game suit." He moves to dodge a spill of juice coming out of the straw.

I have to laugh. "I'm sure you have many other options."

"I do. But seriously, my resolution is that you and I make us work."

Swoon.

"I'm on board with that."

We both glance at the clock on my muted television. Noticing the final countdown, we both begin to whisper the numbers, and when we get to midnight, we clink our juice boxes together and take a sip.

"Happy New Year," he says softly.

"Happy New Year."

Setting the juice boxes on the side table, I climb on top of Tyler to straddle him. The way he looks up at me and I peer down is a magnetism, part of our attraction. My arms encircle his neck, and I press my body down against his warmth.

"Congratulations." I stake his eyes with mine.

"That I'm not getting rid of you?" he retorts.

I hum a sound. "Well, that… but also you survived the holiday season. Mazel tov to you."

He tucks a few strands of my hair behind my ear. "It was only possible because of you, and since we already got through our first holiday season together, then we are already pretty strong, don't ya think?"

I have to smile proudly at our accomplishment and the truth of it all. "Very promising, indeed. Now, should we celebrate?"

His devilish smirk warns me right before he moves and tosses me onto my back on the couch. Being trapped underneath him is the perfect fit. My legs wrapping around his waist is even better.

"I'm following your lead on this. Is it possible to fuck you, because I'm completely crazy about you, or do we need to wait—"

I shut him up with a kiss because I appreciate his respect

for the current house situation with my son down the hall, but I want Tyler. Being quiet when we want to be together on a more intimate level is something that we are going to have to get used to.

"If we have to wait then we'll both lose our minds," I purr into his ear.

"I was hoping you were going to say that," he mumbles, his warm breath cascading down my neck.

Suddenly, the world shrinks around us, and we are the only two people left. I clutch his shirt as he presses a kiss against my lips. My entire body thrums as we simmer together. He balances his weight on one arm because his other hand roams down my body, and his mouth drags down my throat.

Fuck, I love the stubble on his jaw.

My linked legs around his waist pull him closer as if it will relieve the tight curling between my legs, but the feeling of his hard cock only makes it worse. I shiver at the thought of what he is about to do to me. From instinct, my body arches into him the moment his fingers sneak between the fabric of my pajama pants and brush over my soaking panties.

"You are so fucking wet and so fucking mine," he murmurs. The way his fingers yank the fabric to the side and his fingers touch my pussy causes me to release a shaky breath.

I attempt to work on the buttons of his shirt, but he tuts me with his thick voice. "We don't have time for that. I believe the clock struck midnight, and we have to celebrate as soon as possible that you're mine."

This man knows how to send new waves of heat through me.

"Agreed." I'm already breathless.

He owns me with a kiss, our tongues entwining, only to

part because we are in a hurry. We both shift, allowing me to shove my pants down low enough, then quickly begin to work his belt that he assists me with.

Halfway to his knees, he reaches to fish out a condom from his pocket. He came prepared. Creating a little space, I let him handle the condom.

My attention returns when I feel slight relief when the tip of his cock brushes along my inner thigh, and he lets a low curse rumble through his throat. Digging my fingers into his back, I bite my bottom lip because I'm a moment away from having him inside me.

"You're already making me lose my mind," I whisper.

His answer is to guide his cock right inside of me, and I kiss the curve of his shoulder as he pumps into me.

We grind together as we fuck as though we are on a mission, with no need to go slow. Every thrust is torturous, but every second is also rewarding because we are working through our pleasure together.

His breath, laced with his lips dragging along my jawline, causes him to appear desperate for clasping onto every little thing about me. It's sexy as hell, and I smirk briefly to myself.

I can't help but spread my thighs a little wider because his thrusts are blunt, and every movement brings him deeper. I squeeze around him and claw the back of his shirt.

We are nowhere near naked enough, but it doesn't matter; it doesn't deter what we both want.

Our orgasms come quickly, and his groan turns to ragged breathing when I touch his cheek. Then, it takes only a second to stop and look into one another's eyes. My chest rises and falls, but still, I pull him down to rest his head against me and stay seated between my legs. I'm well aware that we can't stay like this for long, but a minute or two this way is fine.

The feel of my fingers threading through his soft hair calms my breathing. Actually, it's Tyler who is responsible for my body being completely sedated and relaxed. He wasn't supposed to be the guy who could do this to me.

But he is.

And a few minutes later when he returns from the bathroom and gets comfortable on the couch, pulling me in close for a cozy cuddle session, I feel lucky.

Because this is the best midnight on New Year's ever.

MY BODY STIRS AWAKE, and the first thing that I feel is my stiff body. Probably because I'm in the most uncomfortable position. I'm groggy and my eyes are barely open, but the moment I stretch my arms out and hit hard warmth, I remember last night. We must have fallen asleep on the couch because daylight is streaming through the blinds.

Sitting up, the throw blanket falls to my waist, and Tyler begins to move slowly.

"Morning," I say drowsily.

He rubs his face as his mouth stretches into a smile. My eyes run up and down his body. His dress shirt is unbuttoned at the top and his collar is up, along with his sleeves rolled and morning stubble on his chin. He's tired but far too attractive still.

"Did we fall asleep on the couch?"

We were talking all night, and it never crossed my mind that we should go to my bedroom, nor that he should go home.

"Yeah," I answer the obvious.

"I should probably go before—"

"Mom?" It seems someone sneaked into the living room.

We both zip our gazes to Enzo in his pajamas standing on the other side of the room. I'm grateful that he seems to have a little more strength and is up and about. His hair is a mess, but that's what makes him adorable to me. Not so thrilled that he just walked in on us, though.

"Feeling better?" I rush up and straight to my son to feel his head and check his body.

"I'm kind of hungry." His chin juts out when he spots Tyler, almost as if he's in disbelief that he is here. "Tyler's here, Mom."

I smile to myself. "I noticed."

"Hey, kiddo, Happy New Year! I fell asleep when I came to talk to your mom. It was late." Which is all kind of true.

I give him a thumbs-up, as Enzo's back is to me.

"That just means you can have banana pancakes with us. My mom always makes them when it isn't a school day."

"Very true, but maybe you should stick with toast for now due to your stomach," I suggest. When he darts his head to me with a glare that seeps straight through me, I've received my warning. "Or you can try one pancake, and we take it from there." His wide cheeky grin appears due to his win. "Why don't you rest on the couch and put on some TV. I'll bring you your breakfast."

Tyler walks toward me. "I'm going to quickly change at home and come back, if you agree with your son's invite."

"I do."

The smolder in his eyes speeds up my heart.

And later, when we are sitting on the floor eating pancakes, and with Tyler ever so often playing footsy with me under the coffee table and my son eating his cut-up pancake on the couch, everything is promising for my future.

CHAPTER 17
TYLER

Not going to lie, walking toward Lainey's brother in the hall of the arena where we just had a game is daunting. Especially since Anaheim lost, which means he will be in a shittier mood.

Since New Year's with Lainey, it's become clear that we are meant to give us a go. I only do things in which I will succeed and that means being the best boyfriend and more on earth. I swear, my mind couldn't even construct that sentence a few months ago.

Maybe my dad rubbed off on me, because I feel the need to go a little old-school and speak with her brother. It's the honorable thing to do. It's better this way because I'm going to give Lainey my jersey, and that could send him over the edge if he doesn't have a warning.

Seb's back is against the painted white brick wall, and his feet and arms are folded. His stoic face means there will be no chitchat. He is in jeans, a shirt, and has showered hair, which means he at least had time to calm down, I hope.

Arriving in front of him, I return the serious expression. "Hey. Thanks for meeting me."

"Trust me. You couldn't have picked a better moment." He's sarcastic.

"Look, I'll be quick. Lainey and I—"

"Yes. You and my sister. I should have put you in the penalty box when I had that opportunity behind the net."

I scratch my jaw and attempt to figure out the best way to approach this. "You're smart. You are aware that we've grown closer."

"No shit. Now tell me this isn't for fun."

"It's not. I mean, at first your sister and I got off on the wrong foot, but then there was Halloween and something shifted. Thanksgiving came and we gravitated to one another. Then there was Jaime's friend—"

Seb's hand darts out to touch my shoulder and stop me. "What?" His tone is sharp.

Ah fuck. She never told him.

I sigh, and his hand drops. "Shit. I thought she would have told you. She ran into her asshole ex's friend who shares the same characteristics."

Fury fills his entire body. "What did he say to her?"

"Nothing. I got him to leave."

Seb stands taller and adjusts his neck and seems to appreciate it, but his face is still cold and contemplating murder. "Good."

I search the hallway and see that there are only a few people packing away equipment at the end. Other than two guys on the team, nobody is aware that Seb's sister and I are together.

"Look, I just wanted to say that I'm serious about Lainey."

"It's not just Lainey."

"Enzo is part of the equation, and I'm on board with that. He's a great kid."

Seb continues to drill his gaze into me. He's completely unreadable. "If you fuck things up, then holy shit there will be hell for you to pay."

I nod gently in agreement. I get it, I do.

"So, what? You came here to ask for my approval?" Now I see the hint of humor laced in his facial expression.

"I'm going to give her one of my jerseys."

"Awww, how cute. Tyler wants to give a girl his jersey," he mocks like I am a child, but then his demeanor changes. "But that traditional BS is a big step." Can this dude give me any indication of what he is feeling?

Rolling my shoulders back, I decide to take control of the situation. "Like it or not, it's happening. I just thought I would give you a heads-up."

He tips his nose a little higher as if he is sniffing out the situation. "Don't get cocky. As much as I fucking hate it, Lainey is Lainey, and although you are a grumpy fucker, you are a stand-up guy. So, fine. But this is my warning that I have no problem with murder."

His icy gaze is in full force when he bumps into my shoulder as he walks away.

At least I can check this conversation off the list.

Drying my hair with a towel, I watch the hockey highlights on the television mounted on the wall. We just got back from our away game, and tomorrow we will head into another practice before our home game the day after. January to February is killer on the hockey schedule.

The adrenaline is on full blast because our team is one spot away in the standing to hopefully get a wildcard spot for the cup. We still have a lot of games to play, but for now, we are in a good place.

But the adrenaline? It's actually because of Lainey in this very moment.

I said I would see her and Enzo for dinner.

Tossing my towel to the side, I slide my cell out of my jeans pocket and swipe the screen to order pizza. It's the easiest. Enzo can be picky, and Lainey shouldn't have to cook after a long day. I choose classic cheese for Enzo and opt for the veggie for Lainey and meat overload for me. After, I check my calendar because I have a call with my agent scheduled for tomorrow.

Something else catches my eye on the calendar. It happens right during all-star week, actually. I've never once taken notice of this particular day except hearing from the guys what they do every year.

February 14th.

Valentine's Day.

Damn. Now that day needs to have an alarm or three on my phone. It is positively insane, but it's also kind of exciting. I can think of ways to surprise Lainey. It's cliché for sure, the whole day, but I want a piece of the experience. I'll just have to think of the best way to celebrate it.

For now, I focus on tonight.

I finish up a few things then open Lainey's apartment door. Normally, I knock. However, I can hear that she's in the midst of a debate with Enzo. I get the gist of it as I work my way through their home.

"Enzo. For the last time, please pick up the cars and zip up your school bag for tomorrow, otherwise I'm swapping your cheese pizza for broccoli and celery sticks with rice." She doesn't mean it, and even annoyed with her son, she has that warm affection for him.

"Tyler!" Enzo stands up from the mess on the floor and runs to me. Lainey's sight follows her son, and she gives me a welcoming but exhausting smile.

I kneel down to be at Enzo's height. "What's going on?"

"That was an awesome assist last night… I mean, Uncle Seb played good, but you played better."

Lainey sets her hands on his shoulders as she stands behind him. "Let's keep that opinion between these four walls," she muses.

"Thanks, buddy. But what's this I hear about not listening to your mom?"

His eyes dip down, with his chin to his chest. "It's too much to clean up."

"That's why we put things away as we play," Lainey reminds him.

"Your mom is right."

She scruffs his hair. "Go work on your room and I'll help with the living room, okay?" Sometimes compromises are best.

"Okay." He runs away.

I'm finally able to stand and pull Lainey into a hug before giving her a long kiss. We only do this when Enzo isn't around. To him, I'm just a friend and neighbor. Going slow for him is understandable, and I follow Lainey's cues.

But the other side of us, I can push.

"Pizza should be here in twenty."

"Perfect." She interlaces our fingers and walks me to the couch to plop us down onto the cushions, and she faces me on her side and rests her head against her propped elbow on the back of the couch. "You must be exhausted. You had a late game then flew out this morning."

"Nah, I'm used to it. Besides, you've had to deal with Hurricane Enzo today."

Her brows rise knowingly. "It's been one of those days." She puffs out a breath.

This is my in. "Then let's just get it all out."

She shifts and seems confused. "Is everything okay?"

I'm leaning leisurely back with my feet planted on the ground, my hands on my thighs, and I turn my head to meet her gaze. "It's perfect. I just wanted to let you know that I spoke with your brother after the game."

She juts her chin out and her eyes are wide. "Oh? And you're here in one piece."

The corner of my mouth stretches from the obvious assumption. "It was good. I just wanted to tell him something before I ask you."

"Ask me what?"

I trap her hand on her thigh between my palms. "You and me. We're doing well, and I will completely follow you when it comes to Enzo. I just want you to know that I'm in this, and I understand that you're not alone but…" What am I saying exactly?

Lainey's eyes narrow, and she tips her head to the side. "You want to go official?" she finishes my sentence because our brains have synced.

"Yeah, you wearing my jersey while in the box with the other players' girlfriends and not hiding." It's completely selfish. "Honestly, I understand that we need to tread carefully for Enzo."

She scoots closer to me. "I love that you are so adamant about it. You care, and I have no doubts about it. Actually…" Her mouths seals then opens with a smile. "I wanted to talk to you about everything tonight. We've been dancing around one another all of fall and winter, and I'm certain of what we are. I think it's time that Enzo knows about us. He's smart."

Wow, I've been waiting for this sign, but now that it's

here, I feel nervous. That takes me off guard but in a good way.

"Okay. How do you want to do this?"

Her hand escapes my palms, and she begins to draw her finger in circles on the back of my hand. In a soothing way. "There is no better time than now. I thought about talking alone with him about it, but last night when I let him stay up late to watch your game, I realized we should do it together. You're already embedded in our life."

I love hearing this. My heart is bursting, and I'm a version of myself that I don't quite recognize.

My other hand cups her cheek, and I press my thumb near the corner of her mouth. Her eyes delicate and face soft. "I love you," I whisper. Maybe it was in the back of my head to say, but right now it spilled out of my mouth because it's a moment that needs truth.

Lainey has a radiant glow, with her wry grin. "I love you too."

We meet halfway when we slowly kiss. Our confirmation of us.

Our mouths part, and my lips trace hers. My breath is warm and my body in bliss.

This woman has the power to make me the opposite of everything I am on the ice. Luckily, I can compartmentalize a little. But off the ice, I'm a goner. A man my father raised and the man that I'm proud of when I look in the mirror because I recognize that my special someone has entered my life, and I won't let her go.

"It's done," Enzo interrupts us, giving us just enough time to create space between one another.

Lainey abandons me on the couch and waves to Enzo, indicating that he needs to sit down on the lounge chair. He doesn't seem fazed and obeys. She then joins him and sits on the arm of the chair.

"Maybe we should wait until after pizza, but I'm going to share something with you now," she tells him. I stay in my spot and let her lead. "Tyler and I, we're more than friends." Enzo doesn't quite understand, it's apparent on his face. "As in the whole boyfriend and girlfriend thing that you hear about from movies and your friends."

"Ohhh." A light clicks on his head. The widest ear-to-ear grin that I've seen in a long time appears, with his missing tooth in full show. "I kind of thought so. This is super cool. Now we can go to games, right? Like, get the cool snacks and shirts."

I try to hide my chuckle because this is a lot easier than I expected, and his concern is food. Lainey's face is priceless, as if she is disappointed that her son just gave her an out for a conversation that she's probably been nervous about.

"Any questions?" Lainey says flatly, as she is still in awe.

Enzo shakes his head. "No."

"Really?" Should I be doubting his confidence in his answers? Is this all a cover to prank me later because he hates the idea of his mom and me together?

"Yeah. Hey, Mom, do I still have to clean up in the living room? Or can I do it tomorrow morning?"

Whoa, the kid is treating this conversation easy as a breeze.

"Ha. Fat chance," Lainey responds, and she seems to be following his signals of keeping this conversation simple. "How about grabbing some plates for me?"

"Fine," he moans and mopes away. "But the cheese pizza is mine."

Lainey gives him a little curtsy that he doesn't see. "Yes, your majesty."

She stretches her neck to watch for him to be out of earshot, and the moment he is, her eyes blaze open, and she looks at me with an ear-to-ear smile. "Sometimes it's better not to make a big deal out of something."

"Oh, because this isn't a big deal," I say, flippant.

She pads over on the balls of her feet to me. "Like I said, you've already been part of our lives, so I guess that doesn't change. We might want to work our way into the whole kissing in front of him or sleepovers. But we no longer need to sneak around."

I yank on her wrist, and she falls straight onto my lap and loops her arms around my neck. "Okay, I can do that. G-rated cuddle time during movie night. Arm around your shoulders while thinking about my hand on your thigh under the blanket."

That sultry look of her comes out to taunt me. "I'll make it up to you, I promise."

"I need examples," I urge.

Her fingers begin to play with the hairs on the back of my neck. "My mouth enjoys being stuffed," she whispers against my cheek before kissing the corner of my mouth.

My hands frame her hips to keep her on top of me. "Inappropriate. It's almost pizza time, and you're trying to make me suffer," I tut.

"I would do no such thing." She curls her lip into a pout. "But I might have something special to wear next time we do end up in bed." She flutters her lashes, and my entire body is about to ignite on fire.

"Your bewitching ways are out in full force today."

She shrugs. "I'm just happy," she replies in earnest. "Now tell me about this jersey."

"It has my number and says boyfriend. It'll drive me

insane when I'm on the ice but will fuel my need to impress and win a game."

Her lips part open in feigned shock. "Tyler Ives, are you using me for your career ambitions?"

I squeeze her flesh, and it causes her to yelp. "That's just a bonus. I have what I need in my lap right now."

Our noses nuzzle, and the feeling of her in my arms with a direction that is only going forward feels like the best goal of my life.

She seals our lips together for a kiss, and we both hum a sound from the feeling of one another, and when our kiss breaks, she drags herself off my body and offers me her hand.

"Come on, boyfriend, it's pizza time, and later I want to try on this jersey of yours."

"A perfect plan." I'm on board with this. "Only my jersey on and nothing else?" I try my luck.

"No need to ask the obvious." She yanks me to hurry.

CHAPTER 18
LAINEY

I'm already untangling the scarf from around my neck as I step off the elevator. February has not been kind to Illinois citizens. Every time I go outside, it takes a few hours to feel my toes again. With the game schedule and moving slow around Enzo, my options for using a bristly hockey player as my heating solutions are limited.

I'm already searching in my purse for my keys and feel exhaustion taking over. Helping little hands paint hearts at preschool drains my energy. Despite the paint smocks, almost all of the class ended up with paint everywhere other than where it was supposed to go. The week of Valentine's is always a mixed bag. It's prime season for kids to be sick with a cold or other bugs. It's also a holiday that has never really been on my radar to enjoy. Enzo has always come first, dating second. I also never wanted the reminder of my solo status. I always stuck to Galentine's celebrations and never ventured further.

This year? It's a struggle to shake what is no longer true. A dislike for Valentine's Day was just too deep inside of me. I'm doing my best to shake it away.

Yawning, I unlock my door with full intention to enjoy an hour or two of calm. Luckily, today wasn't my carpool day for Enzo and his friend's karate class.

The moment I walk through my door, I'm hit with a balloon in my face. I jump, startled, and I bring a hand to my heart while I yelp.

What the hell?

This morning, the team sent chocolates to all the wives and girlfriends of the team, I thought that was my present of the day.

Pushing the balloon angrily to the side, I drop my keys on the side table and quickly hang up my coat, as I'm only confronted with more heart-shaped balloons. Pink, red, more pink. My arm gets tangled in the string of one balloon, and I try to shake it off because I'm annoyed.

Maybe I should be concerned about walking into a home with balloons that I didn't place there, but a burglar wouldn't take his time to cause this fiasco.

The flicker in the bottom of my vision causes me to look down and see candles. Creating a path on the floor in the direction of the kitchen.

"Uhh, okay, I'll go with this," I say aloud. I'm too distracted by the Valentine explosion happening in my house. "Really? Rose petals on the ground?" I grumble.

Following the trail, I reach my destination in the kitchen where a giant heart-shaped box of chocolates is on the kitchen counter, along with a dozen roses and paper confetti scattered around the counter.

Now it's beyond obvious that Tyler is determined to go overboard. Someone did this all in my apartment and it's Valentine's Day. "Tyler?" I know the answer but still feel inclined to ask.

My entire heart sinks straight into my stomach, and I

shriek when he jumps up from behind the other side of the kitchen island holding a bottle of champagne.

"Fuck," I bring my hand to my chest and curl over. "Scare me, why don't you?"

He laughs and grins. "Surprise." Not really. But still, this balloon fest was not on my bingo card.

My heartrate is speeding. "What is this?" I sound a little agitated, I admit. Maybe it's because I already had it in my head that he would forget what today is, and even though it wouldn't bother me, making him squirm is kind of fun. I even went lingerie shopping for the occasion.

He circles around the island, setting his very-expensive-looking bottle of champagne down in the process then comes straight to me and cups my face. So infuriatingly sexy. "It's Valentine's Day, baby." I stare at him, unresponsive, and it only causes him to smirk in satisfaction. "Oh yeah, Miss Cheery December Holidays hates Valentine's Day."

"It's not that I hate it."

"You do," he reminds me firmly. "Hence, why going over the top and adding confetti to piss you off came so easily to me."

I feign shock. "Wanting to piss off your girlfriend for Valentine's Day with actual valentines, huh. At least you didn't get me a teddy bear, because then you will have really gone the extra step to piss me off."

He gives me an overdone smile. "Might want to check your bed later. I just couldn't lead the rose petals there in case Enzo came home early." He makes a funny face. "Gotta keep the kid innocent for as long as we can."

I nod in agreement, but my brows are raised and my face sours. "Come on, really? All of this?"

That devilish chuckle under his breath nearly melts me.

He taps my lips with the pad of his thumb. "Don't be grumpy. You have a reason to enjoy this holiday now."

"With a boyfriend who gets his thrills by planting my equivalent of creepy clowns in my home."

He ignores my dry humor and instead begins to work on the cork of the bottle. "Of course I'm going to take pleasure in this day. You gave me hell for not being bright and chipper for every holiday from October to January first. So yeah, karma is not your friend today."

His confidence right now and my own ridiculousness causes a tiny smile to seep through me. "Better be some damn good champagne."

"I was kind of hoping you would tell me to save the champagne for later and we could go straight to your room since we have a window of opportunity."

That breaks me.

I giggle once, and my cheeks already hurt from my smile. "Is that my cue? Because I didn't know we were doing this Valentine's thing, so I haven't done any special shopping." A lie. My lingerie receipt was beyond average.

Tyler gives up on the bottle and opts to grab my wrists. "I leave no Valentine's stone unturned. I took care of that. You have a box waiting for you next time we have a sleepover."

"Well, didn't you think of everything." I pinch him playfully.

Enzo understands that Tyler sometimes stays over after we watch a movie. But with Tyler's schedule, it hasn't happened much. When it does, absolutely no toys and special lingerie come out. I much rather opt for pajamas in case Enzo needs something during the night.

"Well, I'm going to enjoy every moment of today. Teasing you and punishing you are two of my favorite pastimes, you know."

He tugs me along straight to my bedroom where we collapse on my bed, and I fall onto a white teddy bear. I grab it and throw it to the floor. Tyler takes the opportunity to hover over me, and it feels electrifying.

All smiles and laughs aside, we sink into a moment of quiet, lost in each other's eyes. I tip my mouth up to capture a kiss from him.

And it's everything I want and then some.

"This isn't so bad, is it? Over-the-top hearts. You can add this day to your calendar and get all excited."

I roll my eyes. "Perhaps…" The feeling of him near and my strained cheeks from my joy is what I always imagined this day would be like. "You are right," I reply quietly.

His fingers begin to tickle my side. "What was that? Did you say I'm right?"

I shove him off and roll us so I can straddle him. "Yes. Now you can drop the act. I know you hate this holiday."

He brings his hands behind his head and gets comfortable as he stares up at me. "Meh. It's kind of fun, to be honest."

My eyes bug out, and my mouth parts open. "You just said that?" And he was serious.

He shrugs. "Yeah. I mean, it's kind of fun taking a moment to celebrate the one you love."

I circle my hips around his middle and throw my arms up. "Ah yes, and you love me." I love being reminded of that part.

"And you love me, so here we are. Now will you kiss me, spank me, or go down on me? Because I'm losing it here." He lifts his hips, and I feel his hard bulge.

I give him a sultry smirk. "I guess flowers and chocolates can be rewarded," I rasp. My eyes sink down to watch my fingers crawl up his abs, dragging the fabric of his shirt with them. I'm going slow to antagonize him a tad.

"Remind me to break out the piece de resistance first to avoid this torture that you're putting me through," he says. I stall my fingers just under his chest. "Check under your pillow," he suggests.

Now he has me intrigued again.

I study him for a second because I'm not sure what I will find. My hips stay square to his, but I lean across him to reach under the pillow. In the process, my body brushes along his mouth, and he takes the opportunity to give me a little playful bite.

My fingers search under the case and instantly my body freezes.

It's a key with my name on the keychain. Feels a little more official than the spare key that I use sometimes.

"What's this?" I choke out.

Tyler cooly remains unaffected. "Just your very own key for when you move in."

"Move in?"

He grips my waist and flips us so he is on top. "Yeah. We're long game, and the next step would be living together. I know it might sometimes feel that way because we're neighbors, but we are also not living together. Enzo has to be comfortable, of course. It's just... not living together doesn't feel like enough, you know?"

Every word he just said was dripping warmth and honesty. "I get it. It's crossed my mind. I mean, when the season ends then you are off for months, and will our dynamics change or...?"

Tyler kisses the corner of my mouth, keeping our bodies close. "I mean, if I were to get traded or something, I want you and Enzo with me. If I can't marry you yet, then live with me, it's the next best thing. Maybe you're not ready now, but I'm waiting when you are."

I freeze when I repeat his sentence back in my head. "You want to marry me?" It peeps out.

"Well, obviously that's the game plan, but we said to go slow, so I'm trying to find some middle ground."

"And one day marry me?" I can't let this go.

Why? I'm the queen of slow and responsible decision-making. Filling my head with this thought is neither one of those.

Tyler is unfazed. "I want you guys by my side. Living under one roof is the way to go, and then I can hide a ring in your Halloween candy or something. Not sure I'll make it to the fall holidays. Not sure how I feel about rings stuck in Easter Eggs, either." He's rambling, and it's so perfect.

"Tyler," I whisper his name. He realizes that he needs to give me a moment to speak. "I'm happy to hear about the long-game plans."

"You're on board, right?"

I nod my head. "We're going at our own pace, but all of those things are for us. I want them too," I confirm.

Our mouths fuse together, and we kiss our breaths away. "I love you," I breathe out before we kiss again.

"I fucking love you," he laments before his mouth runs down my neck.

It seems I can add Valentine's Day as a new holiday to like.

EPILOGUE: TYLER

NEXT CHRISMUKKAH

Lainey trudges groggily into her living room in her Hanukkah-themed fleece pajamas that were a gift from my aunt. It's morning, and even though Enzo faced the reality of Santa, he is still eager to open his presents this morning and is sitting on the floor near the tree, shaking a few small boxes.

A few months ago, we found a house that will give us a little more room, plus a yard. We'll be moving in next month after the holiday buzz calms.

Lainey plops onto the couch, and I'm quick to offer her a cup of coffee that I already made because I've been up for an hour for many reasons.

"We have a solid two hours before we head to Chrismukkah at Gracie and Asher's," she mumbles.

"And a solid one minute for you to wake up and get with the show," I retort.

She rolls her eyes and smiles against the rim of her mug.

"Can I open one now?" Enzo is about to lose patience.

"Sure," Lainey agrees.

Truthfully, I barely notice the *wows* happening for the next five minutes from Enzo opening his new dart set and a bunch of hockey stuff. He has a talent and is doing great on the mini-team. It makes Seb and me proud. Seb is relaxed about his sister and me, so things are smooth sailing.

But the real reason why everything feels like it is in the background is the fact that I keep admiring Lainey. My eyes are unable to part from watching her bright smile as she watches her son. But it's time, and before she opens her gifts, I need to get this out of the way because I can't focus.

"Guys, we totally forgot to check our stockings." I play it casual. "Not sure Santa appreciates that."

Enzo sighs as though it is an inconvenience, and Lainey chirps a laugh. "Tyler is right. Stockings should always be the first thing to open."

We all work our way to the fireplace where three stockings are hanging and a menorah that I bought from an actual store rests on the mantel. Last year's Chrismukkah might have rubbed off on me, and Enzo asked as well. Enzo digs into his and pulls out his pair of socks and a few chocolate bars. I went off script and got him a gift card so he can download some games, which causes Lainey to zip her eyes to me, and she wants to be angry, but her smile fails her.

My stocking also has socks and chocolate. Both Enzo and I wait for Lainey, but she does nothing, instead snapping her fingers in the air. "I totally forgot to add your parents' presents under the tree for tomorrow."

She's about to twirl on her feet to fix that situation, but I grab her arm to stop her. "No, you don't. You have a stocking still stuffed."

"Yeah, yeah, yeah. Let me grab my socks and chocolate because Tyler has become Mr. Holiday this year and was on stocking duty." She humors us and stuffs her hand into the stocking, only to pause, and her hand begins to fish around. The expression on her face stalls, and her eyes brighten as she slowly pulls out the small square box. "W-what's happening?" she asks blankly.

Catching her off guard is fun. Confident with what I'm about to do, I drop to one knee. I catch her hands to hold and steal the item in her hand. Opening the box, I present it to Lainey. Already, tears pool in her eyes. "I'm hoping you'll make my Chrismukkah miracle come true this year."

Enzo has a wide smile as he stands by the side. He knew I was going to ask and even came along when I picked out a ring.

"I thought you would get me a necklace with a little charm or something." She is stuck in a daze.

"I did that already on your birthday," I deadpan.

Her mouth parts open and words seem to get stuck. I'm beginning to worry.

"Can you actually ask the question?" she directs me, and my body eases because a smile is breaking out on her face.

"Will you marry me?"

When she pounces on me and throws her arms around me, it causes me to fall back onto my ass and take her with me. "Yes!"

Everything inside of me bursts, a spectrum of emotions that I've never experienced. Sure, winning a cup could be up there on the list, but hockey won't always be there, and Lainey I get for life.

"Let me get that ring on your finger then."

We sit up, and she stays on my lap as I slide the ring onto her finger. She flaps her hand against my shoulder as if she is a penguin, and her blatant excitement is the best. "This is a great start to the day. Now we have family and friends to share the news with."

Oh yeah. *That.*

"Let's go build our safety bunker in your room for tomorrow when my parents visit," I advise. She swats me and laughs. "What? My mom is going to squeal all day, before planning our wedding as if it were her own. And we still have to head to Gracie's later to stare at a baby in an elf hat or something."

She points her finger at me and gives me a pretend stern look. "Hey, not my fault that your coach got my best friend pregnant, and their cute little baby has their first Chrismukkah. Plus, apparently we will be playing a solid game of dreidel with alcohol."

My grin breaks out. "Fair enough. Now let's celebrate over some cinnamon rolls and your disgusting candy-cane-flavored coffee."

She bounces up and off of me and offers me her hand. As we walk to the kitchen, she takes her place between Enzo and me. One fit.

A family of three.

…maybe soon four, if I have my way.

www.ingramcontent.com/pod-product-compliance
Lightning Source LLC
Chambersburg PA
CBHW070653010826
48975CB00013B/1088